GOLD
SECTOR

USA TODAY BESTSELLING AUTHOR
LEXI C. FOSS

Gold Sector

Editing by: Outthink Editing, LLC

Proofreading by: Katie Schmahl & Jean Bachen

Cover Design: Manuela Serra

Title Page Cover Design: Lori Jackson

Forced Edges: Painted Wings Publishing

Published by: Ninja Newt Publishing, LLC

Print Edition

ISBN: 978-1-68530-416-4

AI Disclaimer: This book does not contain any elements of AI content. All art was designed by real artists, and all of the words were written by the authors.

To those who feel they need to hide their true selves.
No matter what others say, you're amazing. You're beautiful. And to
me, you are seen.

I hope you can find safety in this fantasy escape and enjoy Taliana's
journey as she falls for an Alpha who loves her both inside and out.
He doesn't care what society says or what his clan expects of him.

He follows his heart… right to Taliana's nest.

GOLD SECTOR

A DRAKON-CLAN NOVEL

GOLD SECTOR

I'm a broken Omega.
A hybrid wolf shifter
An abomination to dragonkind.
If these Alpha dragons find out, they're going to send me
back to the nomad lands… *to die*.

They already suspect that I'm something "other."
Hence the evaluations and trials laid out before me.

So when my Alpha guard offers me a set of magical gold
coins, I try to use them to buy favor with the Royal Court.
Except they want *more*.

To survive, I strike a deal with my handsome guard—I'll
give him whatever he wants in exchange for more of his
golden enchantments.

There's just one problem.
I underestimated the cost of this agreement.
Because it turns out there's only one thing my Alpha guard
wants.
And it's the one thing I can't give…
An heir.

Author's Note: *Gold Sector* is a "Rumpelstiltskin" retelling
that features a fast-paced, fast-burn plot and a happily-
ever-after ending.

INTRODUCTION

This world isn't kind. It's futuristic and dystopian, and over 90 percent of the human population no longer exists. Supernaturals are in charge here, their territories often referred to as "sectors," where Alphas make the rules and everyone else obeys.

Welcome to Drakon-Clan...
Land of the dragons.
Home of mystic energy.
And a cluster of sectors governed by Alpha Princes.

Below are some themes you may find in *Gold Sector*:
☑ This is a "Rumpelstiltskin" Retelling (or it's loosely inspired by the clever little imp, anyway)
☑ Consent Between Hero and Heroine
☑ Virgin Heroine/Experienced (and patient) Hero
☑ Mentions of Nonconsent/Abuse to Tertiary Characters
☑ No Other Woman or Other Man Drama (No Cheating)
☑ Pregnancy/Breeding
☑ Primal Energy
☑ Possessive Over The Top Alpha Male
☑ Touch Her and Die Vibes
☑ Knotting, Nesting, Purring, Growling

CHAPTER ONE
TALIANA

Follow the rules.
Play your part.
And whatever you do, don't look up.

My father's words reverberate in my head as I try to heed his advice. Moons, it's hard. There's so much energy in this room. So much Alpha *hunger*. My knees yearn to bend, my desire to kneel an intrinsic need that threatens my every step.

Breathe, I tell myself.

Only, that makes it worse.

There are so many competing scents here.

Ash. Pine. Peppermint. Charcoal. Copper. Earth.

I swallow, my fingers curling into fists as I fight the urge to submit more than I already am.

My fate depends on how I'm received here today. How much the Gold Sector Prince feels I'm worth. If he matches me with a Drakon Alpha, then my father will be welcome here, too.

But if the Gold Sector Prince rejects me...

My eyes nearly close at the thought. I can't finish it.

This is my only chance for survival. The alternative is worse than death.

More scents curl around me as I move deeper into the room, and I seek out the only one that offers me some semblance of peace. *The kiss of the ocean.*

It clings to my father's skin, reminding me of home.

If only I could go back there. To a previous time. A previous ruler. A previous… everything.

My limbs shake. *Stop thinking, Tali, and just… walk.*

The cobblestone is cool against my bare feet, my thin dress doing nothing to protect my body from the chilly throne room. Everyone is silent. But their auras are loud. Powerful. *Intoxicating.*

I've met Alphas before—my father is one, too—but I've never felt energy like this. Sizzling. Burning. Enchanting.

Gold Sector is in the heart of Drakon-Clan territory. An island of dragon shifters. Renowned Alpha traders. Possessing a world of secrets.

How my father managed to procure an audience with the Royal Court is beyond me.

I knew better than to ask questions.

All I can do now is try to pay him back by proving to be an Omega worthy of a Drakon Alpha mate.

"State your name and designation," a deep voice booms as I arrive at a gold star etched into the floor. It's exquisite. All sparkles and glamour. If I weren't currently the center of attention in the room, I would consider kneeling to stroke the intricate edges of the design.

Instead, I focus on the words still echoing throughout the oval space.

Such a commanding tone, I marvel, nearly dizzy from it. *Definitely an Alpha. Maybe even the prince himself.*

Clearing my throat, I keep my gaze on the ground as I reply, "Taliana Embers, Omega."

"Obviously," the voice drawls. "An Omega from where? What are you?"

I bite my lip, wincing at the hint of irritation in his tone.

Of course he doesn't like me.

I'm a mutt.

A nomad Omega of mixed origin.

Unworthy.

Unwelcome.

Sectorless.

"Obsidian Sector," my father interjects before I can speak. "She's my daughter."

"And you are?" The boredom underscoring the masculine tone makes me shiver. He's obviously unimpressed. But I suppose that's better than being annoyed or angry.

"Alpha Keegan, Drakon origin." That last part is uttered with reverence, suggesting pride in his Drakon soul. If only I'd inherited his Drakonian traits.

Instead, I'm more like my mother.

A mix of Omega genetics.

An experiment.

An abomination.

"Hmm, I see. So your daughter has Drakon blood inside her." The voice sounds slightly more intrigued now. But I'm not sure if that's a good thing.

The hairs along my arms dance as the air shifts, a slithering sound whispering across the cobblestone. I fight the urge to close my eyes as it nears, the overwhelming scent of a raging campfire tickling my nostrils with every inhale.

Remember the rules, I repeat to myself. *Don't move. Don't react. Don't. Look. Up.*

Clawed feet step onto the star, the golden scales nearly

blending into the pattern below it. Only, the shimmer is too alluring to be mere metal. It's glittering. Magical. *A Drakon Alpha in his dragon form.*

So rare. So beautiful. So utterly majestic.

His warmth overwhelms me as he steps closer, his breath stirring the loose hairs framing my face. He's big. *Huge*, even. I don't need to look up to know that. It's evident in the way he's encompassed all my light, cascading me into this perpetual shadow as he inches closer.

Flames and burning wood are all I can smell now, his scent so intense I begin to feel faint.

Breathe, I coach myself. *Just… just breathe.*

Except every inhale makes my knees shake that much more. I want to bow. To kneel. To *supplicate.*

His presence is too overbearing. Too overwhelming. Too *consuming.*

I stop breathing as he presses his snout to my head and inhales.

Oh, Gods…

My father warned me that the Alphas would circle me. Touch me. Maybe even *taste* me. But his vocal preparations paled in comparison to experiencing a dragon's nearness.

It takes considerable effort not to flinch. To remain utterly still. To let this beast evaluate my presence.

"And what is it that you hope to accomplish today, Alpha Keegan? Why did you request this meeting?" The voice uttering the questions matches the one from earlier, confusing my senses.

I originally assumed the owner of the voice had shifted into the dragon before me. But it seems this Alpha is someone else entirely.

So who is the Drakon Prince? I wonder. *The one issuing inquiries or the dragon?*

"I hope to offer my daughter as a potential Omega mate to whomever you deem worthy of her," my father says, his words expected.

What isn't expected is the masculine chuckle that follows. "You think we need Omegas?" Humor underlines the query, the owner of it becoming known as *Voice* in my head.

"I know you do," my father replies without hesitation. "All Alphas need Omegas."

"Yet you want to sell yours?" Voice counters. "If Omegas are so important, why would you want to barter something so precious? Is she defective?"

I nearly wince at the word, my heart skipping a beat in my chest.

The dragon huffs against my hair. It takes everything inside me not to react as he lowers his snout to my neck and inhales deeply.

"My daughter is not defective. She's a hybrid breed, beautiful, and powerful in her own right. If you give her a chance—"

"A chance?" Voice interrupts, a hint of mockery coloring his tone. "Why the fuck should we give you or her a chance?"

"I'm a Drakon Alpha. My daughter has a right to be considered," my father says, patience underlining each word. Patience I recognize. He's never been one to unnecessarily lose his temper, unlike other Alphas I've known. My father chooses reason over using his fists, and it shows now as he adds, "All I desire is for you to evaluate her as a potential mate."

"In exchange for what?" Voice presses. "Compensation?"

"Protection," my father corrects. "For Taliana."

I almost frown. That's not what we discussed. My

father needs resources to survive on his own. Goods to trade. A way to make a living in the nomad lands of this world.

"And?" Voice demands.

"All I care about is my daughter's safety. I want to see her properly mated, then I'll leave."

I can no longer fight the urge taunting my mouth, my lips curling down. *What are you talking about?* I want to ask him. *You were hoping to exchange my mating for gold.* He told me that. Confided in me his desires. Why isn't he telling the truth now?

"Hmm," Voice hums as the dragon steps back from me with a grunt.

That sound doesn't give me positive vibes.

He no doubt smelled my mixed heritage. Realized I'm not a true dragon. *Discovered my inner wolf.*

My shoulders fall, hopelessness engulfing me.

The wolves won't take me.

The dragons won't either.

Only the abominations of Obsidian Sector want me.

And they don't want me for kind reasons.

They—

"Take her away for evaluation," Voice says sharply, his words shivering down my spine with thunderous authority. "And escort Alpha Keegan to a waiting suite. Once we've properly evaluated the Omega, we'll determine if she's worthy of a match."

My blood runs cold. I know what *evaluation* means. Obsidian Sector was notorious for them.

Pain tolerance.

Knot threshold.

Heat cycle.

I shiver. My father saved me the night before my first scheduled session, the experience one that still gives me nightmares. His urgency. His fear. His command to follow.

We ran hard. Fast. In a blur of darkness.

Then he gave me my first suppressant.

A pill that became my weekly regimen for three years.

Until last month when I took the final dose.

Will the Drakonians find any lingering effects in my blood? I wonder as two Alphas flank me, their scents making me dizzy all over again.

Suppressants are typically considered illegal among Alpha kind. They don't like Omegas masking their true natures. But it was a necessity for my father and me to survive in the nomad lands.

If I hadn't run out of pills, we wouldn't be here today.

"You need an Alpha who can keep you safe," my father told me three weeks ago. Then he announced his decision to present me to the Gold Sector court.

I fought at first, determined to find another way.

However, the fight was short-lived.

Because what choice do I have? I'm an Omega. I will go into heat. My first one, too. And it will be soon.

Better here where an Alpha might claim me as a mate than in Obsidian Sector.

Or worse, in the nomad lands.

Although, those last two seem like rather similar fates in my book.

"Omega," a deep voice says, drawing my attention to the male on my left. I nearly meet his gaze, then remember where I am and who I am and instantly drop my focus to the ground.

"Is there a problem, Omega Taliana?" Voice asks, a hint of irritation lurking in his tone.

Moons. He must have said something while I was reacting to the news regarding my *evaluation*.

Clearing my throat, I reply, "No problem, Alpha. Er, Your Majesty?" The formal address comes out awkward, as I'm not even sure Voice is the Gold Sector Prince. But who else could he be?

A long pause follows, one that causes the hairs along my arms to dance.

Someone clears a throat—Voice, maybe? It sounds close to me. Loud. A bit harsh. *I wish I could lift my head.*

"Go with Savan," Voice demands, his words underlined with impatience.

I nod on impulse even though I have no idea who Savan is. I hope he's one of the two Alphas flanking me because I move as they turn and follow them out of the throne room.

When Voice doesn't call after me or shout another command, I marginally relax.

Then I remember where I'm heading, and my shoulders stiffen once more.

An evaluation.

My father warned me this would happen. It's all part of the Omega verifying process.

"They'll be a lot less intrusive than the Obsidian Sector Alphas," he told me. "I wouldn't let them take you if I didn't think this was the best option, Tali."

I believe him.

Or I want to, anyway.

But the lingering scents of fire and ash in the air do little to dispel my nerves.

Nerves that reach a boiling point as we step into an elevator made of gold and head downward.

My fingers curl into fists as the sensation of going underground crawls across my skin, the chill instantly chasing the warmth of being closer to the sun.

By the time the golden car stops, I can hardly breathe.

It's suffocating down here, walking amongst the beings of death.

Wolves thrive above ground.

At least, I do.

Beneath the surface, I can't feel the stars. The moon. *Inhale the sky*.

A palm touches my lower back, urging me out of the elevator. There are words exchanged between the two Alphas, but I don't hear them. My heartbeat is too loud. And my footsteps resemble concrete blocks hitting the marbled floor.

By the time we reach the examination room, I can barely see.

It's all just white.

Sterile.

Reeking of bleach.

I close my eyes and try to focus, try to be a good Omega, to leave a decent impression behind and try to win a Drakon Alpha mate.

This isn't just about me, I remind myself. *It's about Dad.*

He may not have mentioned his desire for gold, but I know he needs it. Which means I have to pull myself together and do this for him.

I steal a deep breath, my nose curling at the stench of cleaning supplies.

You can do this, Tali.

I force my eyes open and take a step inside the small room.

You can do this.

My wooden legs move with a stiffness I feel through every inch of my being.

Just a little more.

I reach the examination bed and note the paper dress waiting for me on top of the white sheet.

"Strip and put on the gown," a gruff voice says from behind me. "Doctor Taylor will be with you momentarily."

The door slams behind me with a finality that leaves me shaking in the too-quiet room, the sound of a lock twisting into place solidifying my fate.

There's nowhere to run. Nowhere to hide. My days as a free Omega have officially come to an end. And the evaluation is about to begin.

.

CHAPTER TWO
OROS

"WHAT DO YOU THINK?" ONYX ASKS AS I SHIFT BACK INTO my human form.

I don't answer my brother right away, instead disappearing behind my throne—the one he's currently lounging on like he's the Prince of Gold Sector—to pull on a pair of black pants.

His silver eyes are on the court's ornate double doors as I round the massive chair made of solid gold. For a moment, I follow his gaze, wondering what he's listening to in the corridor beyond. His hearing has always been better than mine. It's one of his many talents.

Of course, I have my own talents as well.

Such as my ability to smell truths and lies.

"They're hiding something," I tell my brother, answering his question regarding what I think. The *of the Omega and her father* part was implied. "The Omega's scent changed when her father said all he wanted was her protection. She also didn't seem all that keen on being evaluated."

The latter I suspect stemmed from some type of abuse.

Our evaluations are rather standard, the focus being on physical and mental health. But I know not all sectors operate like ours does.

"Obsidian Sector," I mutter, recalling what Alpha Keegan said about where his daughter was from. "He never said *what* she is, though. Just insinuated that she's Drakonian since she's his progeny."

"Well, that makes her at least half Drakonian," my brother points out.

"Indeed," I agree. "But she doesn't smell like a dragon."

Instead, she reminded me of a meadow full of wildflowers. Her alluring scent still lingers in the room, a pleasant aroma that oddly placates my inner beast.

I've met hundreds of Omegas before.

Been with a few through their heats.

Yet none of them ever calmed my dragon.

"No, she reeked of mutt," Onyx growls, causing my shoulders to stiffen. "She's a hybrid, which isn't unexpected given her origin. But what did they pair her with?"

I frown. "She smells bad to you?"

"Not bad, just tainted," he returns. "Why? How does she smell to you?"

"Refreshing," I admit, glancing toward the doors she walked through several minutes ago. The rest of the court followed, leaving my brother and me to speak in private.

A typical session with an outsider—me in dragon form, my brother on my throne, and our trusted generals awaiting our command. Two took Alpha Keegan to a waiting suite. Two escorted the Omega to her evaluation. And the other four are likely in the corridor, guarding the doors but not listening in on our conversation.

"Refreshing," my brother echoes. "That's… an interesting description."

"Is it?" I ask, feigning innocence as I call upon my magic to clothe my torso in my usual armor—enchanted gold.

My brother is similarly dressed, only his metal looks silver in nature because his affinity is for white gold, not yellow gold. Hence his silvery eyes.

Mine are yellow gold in contrast.

"You're interested," he says, sounding surprised. "Dozens of Omega mate offerings and it's a mutt that calls to your dragon?" He whistles. "That beast always was fucking complicated."

"First of all, I never claimed to be interested." A fact, not a lie. "And second, stop referring to the Omega as a *mutt.*" That final word barely escapes my clenched jaw, the term really pissing off my dragon.

A fiery energy stirs, one I know better than to provoke. I may be one with my beast, but his instincts are not always easy to control. Even instincts I don't fully understand.

"I'm going to go observe the Omega's evaluation," I decide out loud, needing to understand my dragon's interest.

Perhaps Taliana possesses some sort of mating energy or a magnetic pull. I'll have to mention the possibility to Doctor Taylor.

Returning to my throne, I put on a pair of slipper-like shoes and grab my cloak to hook it to the gold adornments on my shoulders.

Traditional Drakonian garb. We all show off our metallic gifts, primarily to remind others of our power.

Gold marks me as a royal—my brother, too.

His armor flashes in the light as he ashes to stand before me, blocking my path to the door. "Aren't you forgetting something?"

I glance down at my attire, frowning. "A blade?" I

sometimes carry a dagger on my hip, but it's not a necessity since I can conjure one at will.

"A certain meeting?" he presses, his arms folding over his mostly bare chest.

I consider my schedule for a moment and curse. "Riordan."

"Yes, that would be the one," my brother drawls. "I highly doubt the Alpha Prince of Jasper Sector will appreciate a last-minute schedule change."

My jaw clenches again. Onyx isn't wrong. Riordan isn't exactly known for his patience or his understanding nature.

Oh, he's a fantastic ally.

But a colossal pain in my ass otherwise.

"Can you take the call without me?" I ask Onyx. "It's about trade routes."

"I know what it's about," he replies, giving me a look that says he's a bit offended by my meeting-topic clarification. "Tell me what you're thinking."

I frown at him. "You know how I feel about the negotiation. If he wants access to the Black Sea, then I want access to Gibraltar."

He rolls his eyes. "I meant about the Omega, Rumpelstiltskin. You know better than to leave me on a call alone with Riordan, yet you're risking me jeopardizing our diplomatic relations for a female you just met. I want to know what you're thinking."

"I'm thinking it's time for you to get over your little rivalry with Rio and grow a pair, Silverstiltskin," I retort, throwing the nickname at him in retaliation for him calling me *Rumpelstiltskin*. It's been an ongoing joke between us since we were kids. But sometimes he uses the name to goad me.

Which is precisely the purpose now.

I can see the intent in his glittery irises.

"She's under your skin. Is it her scent? Her curvy little body? That waterfall of silver-black hair?" He runs his gaze over me like he's evaluating a test subject. "I know it wasn't her eyes since she never looked up from the ground. So I'm guessing tits and ass."

My beast growls a little inside me, disliking the crude analysis. Or maybe my dragon is reacting to the combative energy pouring off my brother. "Are you trying to challenge me for her?" I wonder aloud. "Is that what this is?"

His eyes widen, all playfulness disappearing from his features. "Shit, I was joking, but this Omega really does have you by the knot, doesn't she?"

My jaw ticks. "I don't even know her, Onyx," I grit out.

"And yet, you're throwing off waves of possessiveness the entire fucking sector can probably feel right now."

I fold my arms over my still-bare chest, the magical gold adorning my shoulders and biceps flexing and shifting with the movement. "I want to oversee the Omega's evaluation to determine what she's hiding. It's my job to protect this sector, and that means knowing and understanding everything and everyone within my boundaries. Now, will you handle the call with Riordan or not?"

My brother stares at me for a long beat, then nods. "Fine. But I'm not letting him in the Black Sea."

I shrug. "That's between you and Rio now." I turn toward the door, only for my brother to appear before me in a glittery cloud of silver that almost instantly evaporates around his corporeal form.

"Hold on," he says slowly. "Is that what this is? You're feigning interest in the Omega so you can pawn off Riordan on me?"

My lips curl, the notion one that pleases me. "Maybe. Did it work?" I ask him.

I vanish into thin air before he can reply and ash myself down to the lower levels of the building. Despite being several floors below my brother, I can almost hear his string of curses.

Did I intentionally leave him to deal with Riordan? No. Am I sorry that's exactly what I just did? Also no.

Onyx and Riordan have always bickered, their personalities too well matched for them to ever become true allies. But Riordan has his uses, and I'm rather certain he feels similarly about my younger brother.

They just need to work out some of their... kinks.

Good luck, Silverstiltskin, I think, grinning. We can't communicate telepathically, but his voice seems to linger in my mind, taunting my every step toward the labs on this level.

One question in particular haunts me, the words swirling on repeat through my thoughts.

"This Omega really does have you by the knot, doesn't she?"

Does she? I wonder as her scent curls around me like a welcome kiss. *Maybe.*

A strange sensation, one I'm almost certain is the result of some sort of enchantment.

Hopefully, Doctor Taylor will be able to provide more insight.

I turn the corner, nearing her examination quarters, and almost collide with Savan. He jumps back with a curse, his dark eyes finding mine and then flicking away an instant later. "Sorry, My Prince," he mutters, shaking himself.

"What's wrong?" I ask, searching the hallway for the

source of his agitation. Because he's practically huffing, his inner beast clearly ruffled by something.

"The Omega," he grinds out, his teeth clenched. "She's terrified."

My brow furrows. "Terrified of what?"

But as soon as the question is out, I hear her whimper. It's soft. So soft that it barely carries. However, it's the clearest sound in the world to my senses.

I move around Savan and open the door without knocking.

And find Taliana stark naked on the examination bed.

My lips part, stunned by the sight. Then fury quickly replaces my shock as I see her tiny hands curl into fists, her eyes squeezing shut.

Terrified is an understatement.

Fuck.

"Where's Doctor Taylor?" I demand, then wince as the Omega visibly trembles.

"She's gathering all her supplies, My—"

"Tell her I'll call her when we're ready," I reply, cutting off Savan before he can finish his formal address. The last thing Taliana needs right now is to hear my title. She's obviously upset enough. "Take a walk, Savan," I add before shutting the door.

The Omega can no doubt sense his agitation, as well as mine. Drakonian Alphas are designed to protect, and this female is clearly in need of safety. Savan's inner beast is likely rioting right now with the intrinsic desire to destroy whatever has this woman so spooked.

Only, I suspect it's *us* she fears.

Which makes it an impossible task to annihilate the threat.

At least in terms our dragons understand.

No, this is going to take a careful touch.

Leaning back against the door, I evaluate the shivering woman, my brow furrowing. "Where's your patient gown?" I finally ask her.

It's such an inane question. But I'm hoping it'll entice her to speak.

Her slender throat bobs, drawing my attention to her collarbone and down—

No.

I force my gaze back to her chin and then to her full lips as she whispers, "I know it's not needed, so I opted not to wear it."

My eyebrow arches upward. Not that she sees it. Her eyes are still closed. "Why isn't it needed?"

"Because I know what's expected of me." She spreads her legs slightly, the movements rigid and not at all sensual. Yet my gaze is drawn to the apex between her thighs on instinct, her scent hitting me with dizzying power.

Now it's my turn to swallow because *fuck*, she smells amazing. It takes centuries of restraint to force my attention back to her beautiful face.

The worry etched into her angelic features is enough to ground me in the moment and sharpen my focus. "And what's expected of you?" I ask, already dreading the answer.

I can only imagine the horrors she experienced in Obsidian Sector, otherwise known as the infamous land of genetic experimentation.

"You'll need to ensure I can take a knot." She utters the words with resigned conviction, like she's accepted her fate and isn't afraid of it.

Except I can smell her fear.

"You've been evaluated before?" I guess aloud, my voice holding a note of disgust to it. Not because she's been knotted before, but because she was very likely knotted against her will.

Her lashes flutter as her eyes open, a pretty blush stealing over her cheeks. "No, I'm untouched." She glances toward me, then freezes upon meeting my gaze.

Midnight, I think, admiring the color of her irises. *A black sky dotted with silver stars.*

Flames, I've never seen eyes like hers. So illustrious. So unique. So fucking beautiful.

"Are you here to knot me, Alpha?" she asks, her voice tinged with a breathy quality that almost suggests she's interested.

Yet beneath that breathy sound was a tremor of terror, telling me everything I need to know about this situation.

"No," I inform her, instantly snapping into my protector role. "I don't fuck unwilling women."

She flinches, her glorious eyes leaving mine as she looks away in shame. "I'm sorry for displeasing you, Alpha."

Fuck. My tone clearly conveyed my displeasure, but it wasn't for the reasons she thought.

Shaking my head, I start toward her and reach for the cloak at my back. The gold automatically releases it, my mind controlling the metal just as easily as I control my steps.

Taliana's hypnotic gaze flies to me when I'm less than a foot away, her body stiffening like she anticipates some sort of punishment.

But all I do is drape the black fabric over her exposed body.

"I don't know what you've been told, but the Alphas of Gold Sector value consent," I say. "We cherish our Omegas here, and we certainly don't punish them."

Unless it's for fun.

However, I don't add that last bit out loud, as I doubt this female would understand that kind of kink.

She says nothing, probably because she's breathing too hard to speak.

No wonder Savan was in a state, I think, my own dragon pacing angrily inside me. I tasked Onyx with talking to her father. However, I'm absolutely taking that task back. Because I have questions.

Starting with *Who the fuck hurt your daughter?*

Because if it was him, I would kill him without hesitation.

I meant what I said—Omegas are cherished here.

Oh, we have a reputation to the contrary, our missions of stealing Omegas from other sectors renowned throughout the world.

But we only take Omegas who need to be rescued.

And then we help them heal.

The other Drakonian sectors are all aware of our purpose here, which means Keegan knows that as well. So perhaps that's why he brought his daughter here—because he knows she needs to be saved.

So why not start with that? I wonder, admiring the female's slender throat.

"Do you want a Drakonian mate?" I ask her, curious as to whether or not she's actually here willingly. "Or is your father forcing you to be here?"

CHAPTER THREE
TALIANA

THE ALPHA'S QUESTIONS ECHO THROUGH THE STERILE room, his tone demanding answers. Or maybe it's just his commanding presence that makes me feel the need to obey every word.

He's powerful.

I can feel it in his aura, taste it in his scent.

Gods, he smells good. Like a calming fire on a chilly night. Burning wood, the kind my father used when trying to keep us warm in the nomad lands.

That must be why this Alpha's cologne puts me somewhat at ease—he reminds me of a time when I was content and safe.

But he's asking about my father.

Asking if I want a Drakonian mate or if my dad forced me to be here.

"No," I tell the Alpha, the word coming out with a little more force than I intended. However, I can't let him think badly of my father. "He brought me here first. To… to offer me as an Omega."

"That doesn't sound very willing," the Alpha mutters, causing me to look at him again. It's a bold move on my part—meeting the gaze of an Alpha—but I need him to believe me. To *listen* to me.

"I'm an Omega, Alpha. I can take a knot."

"That's not what I asked."

"Then what are you asking?" I demand and almost instantly wince when I realize I'm stepping outside of my role. "I'm sorry, Alpha. I—"

He catches my chin, effectively halting my words, and forces me to meet his gaze again. "Do you want to be here?"

I swallow, uncertain of how to answer that. Not with him so close to me. And... and obviously angry. Right? I mean, he has to be angry. I talked back to him. Alphas don't usually like that. My father is a bit of an exception, as he's always been indulgent where I'm concerned.

Or, well, that's what other Alphas have said, anyway.

He's always encouraged me to speak my mind. Yet he warned me to obey the Alphas of Gold Sector. To not meet their gazes. To not question their authority. To... to play my part of a—

"Taliana," the Alpha says, my name on his lips sounding somewhat foreign.

No, not foreign... *erotic.* I like the way his subtle accent curls around my name, making me sound exotic. Unique. *Beautiful.*

I'm not quite sure how to define his lilt. It's nothing like I've heard before in the nomad lands. Maybe a bit Greek?

Although, I don't know what *Greek* actually sounds like. But this land—*Gold Sector*—used to be a Greek Island. *Santorini*, my father once told me. He's old enough to remember a time when Greece existed, his birth well preceding the Infected Era.

A time when humans ruled the world and supernaturals lived in secret among them.

Then the zombielike plague hit and wiped out most of mortal kind, as well as several supernaturals, too.

I have no idea what it was like to live back then, just the stories my father has shared with me.

"Taliana," the Alpha says again, making me shiver. His grip loosens on my chin, his thumb leaving to trace my jaw. "Do you want to be here?"

There's a gentleness to his tone that confuses me. *Is he angry or not?* I wonder, searching his gold eyes. *He doesn't look angry.* He seems calm. Concerned, even.

"Does it matter what I want?" I ponder aloud, somewhat confused by his question.

"Yes. Very much."

"Why?" I ask him.

"Because we value consent here, and if your father brought you here against your will to mate you off, I need to know." A subtle hint of dominance flows through his words again, one that accentuates his commanding presence. It makes me want to confide in him.

Yet I don't even know his name.

I can't trust him.

But I also don't want to risk him thinking poorly of my father.

I need the Drakonian Alphas to accept me as a potential mate and provide my father with a handsome reward. *So he can survive in the nomad lands.*

Or maybe even… be allowed to stay here. With me.

Clearing my throat, I try to answer this Alpha's question by saying, "My father wants what's best for me."

Those golden eyes flare while he stares down at me, his touch leaving my chin as his hand falls to his side. I suddenly feel a bit cold despite the cloak covering my body from neck to toe. *Why did he do that?* I wonder, still surprised by the gesture. The fabric is warm and smells like burning embers, *like Alpha.*

It has my wolf purring inside, content to be surrounded by such a soothing cologne.

Only my father has ever made me feel safe like this. Strange that an Alpha I barely know has the same impact.

"And what did your father say is best for you?" the Alpha asks.

I chew on my cheek, considering how to respond to that.

"The truth, Taliana. I need to understand why you're really here."

My brow furrows. *What kind of statement is that?* He knows why I'm here—to be evaluated for a mate.

Unless...

"Were you not at the assembly today?" I ask, confusion coloring my tone. "Wait, who are you?" Should he even be in here with me? "You're not the doctor..." I don't phrase it as a question, but as a statement.

He said something about the doctor before, asking where the doctor was, but his voice and presence distracted me from considering what that meant. Or considering the relevance at all. But now—

His palm circles my throat, the touch hot and demanding against my flesh and capturing every ounce of my attention.

"Breathe, Omega," he demands, his thumb running up and down the column of my neck. "*Inhale.*"

I shudder as his order rolls through me, forcing me to obey, to supplicate, to... to... *Oh.* My eyes nearly fall shut when sweet relief hits my senses as air fills my lungs.

"Good girl. Now exhale for me," he says, his voice

warming my skin, his nearness something my wolf welcomes more than she should.

My limbs tingle from following his command, my insides seeming to calm.

At some point… I… I began to panic. Which isn't like me. I survived Obsidian Sector and the nomad lands. What makes Gold Sector so different?

Why am I so nervous here?

Because I know they're going to judge me for being a wolf.

Then they won't accept me as an Omega mate.

And I'll be forced back into the nomad lands… *without suppressants*.

"My name is Oros," the Alpha says, his tongue rolling over the *r* of his name to give it a sensual appeal. "And yes, I attended the *assembly*, as you called it. And no, I am not the doctor. I'm here as your guardian. Nothing more."

I blink at him. *Guardian?* That… that seems like a strange term. Yet rather than questioning it, I find myself asking, "Is 'Oros' Greek?"

His lips curl, causing the defined features of his too-handsome face to melt from aristocratic in nature to an expression of pure amusement. "No, little diamond. It's Romanian."

"Oh." I'm not quite sure where Romanian comes from. My knowledge of previous countries and locations is limited to what my father has shared with me.

The Alpha—*Oros*—strokes my neck once more, then removes his touch. "Are you here willingly, Taliana? Or is your father forcing you to take a mate?" His voice is soft again, but his gold irises glitter with knowledge. Intensity. *Power*.

He's muting his energy somehow, allowing me to

continue meeting his gaze, but I can sense the vitality swirling around him.

This is no ordinary Alpha.

Of course, he's a dragon shifter. And not just any dragon shifter, a *Drakonian*. Just like my father. Only, Oros puts my father's energy to shame. Which is saying a lot, given how powerful my father is in beast form.

"My father arranged this meeting so I can find a mate. He's not forcing me to be here, but I also don't have a choice," I tell Oros, the truth just sort of falling from my mouth. "I'm an Omega living in the nomad lands. I... I need a mate."

"For protection," Oros says, nodding. "I see." He glances over me. "How old are you, Taliana?"

"Twenty-one."

His eyebrows lift slightly. "You survived three years of estrous cycles... without a knot?"

Moons, I've said too much. Yet I've barely said anything at all, and he's already driving straight to the heart of why I'm really here. *I ran out of suppressants, and now my heat is imminent. So I don't have a choice. I need a mate.*

But I... I can't tell him the suppressant part. It's forbidden to use medication to stall an Omega's heat. The Drakon Alphas won't approve. They'll probably shun me for it.

And I'm already going to suffer their ire when they realize I don't have an inner dragon.

"You claimed you're untouched," Oros presses. "That means you've never been knotted, yes?"

"Yes," I whisper. "But I'm an Omega. I can take one. However, I know you'll need to... to confirm that."

"I already said I don't fuck unwilling women, Taliana," he says, folding his arms over his mostly bare chest.

I... I didn't notice before, too lost in his gaze and

presence to really admire his Alpha form, but he's quite chiseled. He's also adorned in a unique golden armor that appears to be glued to his skin.

His chest moves on a slow exhale, the motion highlighting the contours of his pectorals and biceps.

Yes, this is a very good-looking Alpha.

"All right." His tongue twirls across the *r* like it did when he told me his name, causing my focus to go to his mouth. "Let's start over, okay?"

"Start over?" I echo, meeting his gaze again.

"Yes. Today's exam isn't about your ability to take a knot. It's an evaluation of your overall health. A lot of Omegas come to us in an injured state. All Doctor Taylor is going to do is administer a health-related exam. Not a *knotting* exam."

"Oh." I swallow, my brow furrowing. "Okay…"

"You sound uncertain."

"Well, yes. I… I've been told by other Omegas about the evaluations, and they never mentioned health-related exams?" It comes out as a question because I'm still not sure what that means. I'm a hybrid wolf-dragon mix. I don't really get hurt. What's the point of evaluating my health? "Do you mean fertility?"

That would make more sense.

Or… or something to do with… with labs.

Oh, moons. Maybe—

"No. I mean your actual health," he interjects before my mind can wander. "Your physical and mental health, Taliana."

I blink at him. *Mental health?* "You think there's something mentally wrong with me?"

Because he can sense my hybrid state? I wonder, swallowing.

He chuckles. "No. Actually, I think you're quite refreshing, little diamond. But as I said, we take in a lot of

Omegas in various states of distress. So our doctors typically evaluate each case to determine if any medical intervention is needed."

"Various states of distress," I repeat out loud. That isn't exactly how he phrased it before. But the word choice doesn't really matter. All I want to know is "What exactly does that mean?"

He considers me for a moment. "I tell you what—I'm going to go get Doctor Taylor, who is a Beta female, by the way, not an Alpha with a knot. And you can ask her that question. I think she would be better suited to explain our arrangements here in Gold Sector."

I… I don't know how to respond to that. Because it just provokes more questions.

A Beta female doctor?

What do you mean by arrangements?

"Can I introduce you to Doctor Taylor?" he presses when I don't respond.

"Um, yes?"

He frowns. "That doesn't sound very certain, Taliana."

"I don't feel very certain about anything right now, Oros," I retort. Then wince when I realize I'm misbehaving again. "Sorry, Alpha. I—"

"An apology isn't needed," he says, cutting me off. "I like your sass, Omega. It's far more interesting than your submission. At least, in terms of conversation." He winks at me while I gape at him, then steps away. "I'll be back in a minute."

The door shuts before I can comment.

I sit up, causing the cloak to fall to my lap. "What a strange Alpha," I whisper to myself. "A very strange, very good-looking Alpha guardian."

Whatever that means, I think, swallowing as I study the door.

I hope it means he intends to stay close to me while I'm here.

Because I already miss his scent.

An interesting realization, given that I barely know him. But he placated my wolf.

And I very much want to experience that sensation again soon.

CHAPTER FOUR

OROS

"YOU WANT ME TO DO WHAT?" TAYLOR SAYS, INCREDULITY coloring her tone.

I stare down at the petite brunette I often refer to as my best friend and arch a brow. "You heard me just fine, Tay."

"Oh, I heard you. I just don't understand. Why am I lying to the Omega?"

"I didn't ask you to lie."

"You told me to tell her you've been assigned as her guardian."

"Which isn't a lie," I point out. "I protect everyone in Gold Sector."

Tay's long black lashes flutter as she blinks a few times. "And why can't she have a real guardian?"

"Why can't I be a real guardian?" I counter.

"Because you're the Prince of Gold Sector."

"Which makes me the best guardian of them all," I tell her. "As I already said, I protect—"

"Everyone in Gold Sector, yeah, yeah." She waves me off.

If she were anyone else, I would growl.

But because it's Tay, I simply smirk.

And Tay hates it when I smirk.

"Ugh, that face," she grumbles, causing my smirk to melt into an amused grin. "What game are you playing, Rumpel?"

"It's not a game," I reply, ignoring the urge to curse in response to that ridiculous nickname. She learned it from my brother decades ago and uses it whenever she wants to goad me.

"Then why are you volunteering to be an Omega's guardian?" she demands, her hands on her slender hips. "You've never taken an interest in any of our other intake cases, including the ones you brought to me yourself. So why this one?"

My jaw ticks.

I can't answer that question because I don't know the answer to it. So all I can say is "It's my prerogative as Prince of Gold Sector to take on the position of guardian whenever I want. And I don't have to explain myself."

Her black eyebrows jump into her matching hairline. "Seriously? You're going to pull that royal crap on me? Right after asking me for this favor?"

"It's not a favor so much as a directive," I mutter, palming the back of my neck.

"Now you're just asking me to kick your ass."

I snort. "Like you could."

"Oh, I could," she says, poking me in the chest with her perfectly manicured finger. "I have before."

"When I was drunk off of a flame ball." I fold my arms over my chest. "Why are you giving me shit about this?"

"Because this isn't like you at all."

"And?" I press.

"And… and I want to know why," she replies, shrugging. "Consider me nosy."

I narrow my gaze. "Onyx put you up to this, didn't he?"

"No." She frowns. "But now I'm even more curious because that means he's also noticed this strange behavior."

"There is nothing strange about me wanting to protect an Omega. I'm an Alpha. It's what Alphas do."

"Okay, yeah," she agrees. "But to be a guardian?"

"Are you going to help me or not?" I ask, exasperated by this ridiculous conversation. "I'm trying to help the Omega, Tay. Surely you, of all Drakonians, can appreciate that?"

Her teeth clench together audibly. "Low blow, Rumpel. Low blow."

She's not wrong. But I stand my ground. "Please, Tay."

"And now you're begging?" She shakes her head, sending her curls bouncing. "Damn, I need to meet this Omega. She's clearly riddled with magic."

"She might be," I admit. "She certainly smells enchanting."

Tay's eyebrows jump up again, then she laughs. "Wow, how the mighty have fallen. All those poor Omegas in waiting."

"*Tay.*" I can't mask the impatience in my tone, nor do I try. I'm tired of our verbal sparring. "There's an Omega in the other room who is currently cowering under my cloak because she thought this evaluation included a knotting test."

My best friend winces. "Ouch."

"For you, maybe."

She scoffs at my poor attempt at a joke. "That's not

what I meant. But yes, also that." She winces for an entirely different reason now.

My lips twitch. "Careful. Thinking about knots too much might make Sheila jealous."

Tay's eyes light up at the mention of her mate's name, but then darken as she translates my words. "You know, for a man who wants my help, you sure do have a way of pissing me off."

"It's a skill I mastered decades ago," I drawl.

"More like centuries ago," she retorts, then shakes her head again. "All right, Rumpel, I'll play along and name you as her guardian."

"And not tell her my official title," I add.

"And *omit* your title, yes," she agrees. "But you're going to owe me a favor."

"Hmm," I hum, energy spinning between my fingertips as I create a token with my signature stamp on it. The gold glimmers in the bright lights of Tay's office when I flip the piece in the air. She catches it with ease, her dragon blinking in and out of her dark eyes in a show of approval.

"Well, that was almost too easy." She pockets the item. "I'll absolutely be calling in this favor at the most inopportune time ever. You've been warned."

I roll my eyes. "Whatever. Can we go talk to Taliana now?"

"Sure." She grabs her tablet—the one she'll use to scan Taliana for any internal injuries or traumas—and practically skips out the door.

Shaking my head, I follow her through the white corridor back to the examination room. But as we reach the entry, I ash in front of her to take the lead and knock to announce my return.

Tay says something behind me that I don't hear because my gaze is on the half-naked Omega.

She's sitting up with the cloak in her lap, not seeming to care at all that her tits are exposed.

Well, at least she's not lying on the table with her legs spread in anticipation of being knotted.

I clear my throat as I enter, causing the Omega's gaze to instantly meet mine.

The meek female from the Royal Court earlier seems to have disappeared. Now she's having no problem holding an Alpha's gaze, while before she was too fascinated by the floor to bother looking up.

Or perhaps her father instructed her to submit.

Regardless, I'm thankful she's looking at me now so I can stare into her gorgeous eyes. *Like flying at night,* I marvel, momentarily at a loss for words.

Then Tay clears her throat behind me, prompting me to move. "Taliana," I murmur as I walk toward her. "I would like you to meet Taylor. She's the doctor I told you about, and she'll be administering your exam."

Taliana's gaze doesn't leave mine for a beat, her shoulders seeming to tense. Then she inhales, and a note of contentment steals across her pretty features. "Okay."

I smile, pleased that she appears to be a bit more relaxed than before. "She'll also tell you about our Omega relocation program," I add, more for Tay's benefit than Taliana's. "And she'll give you insight into what to expect here in Gold Sector."

Taliana nods. "Okay," she repeats.

"Okay," I echo, winking at her. "Then I'll leave you two to get acquainted."

I take a step back, only for the Omega to make me pause with a "*Wait!*"

I meet her pretty gaze again, somewhat confused. "Are you still worried about the evaluation?"

"Yes. Well, no. I mean…" She visibly shakes herself. "You're leaving?"

"I assumed you would like some privacy for your exam," I hedge, glancing between her and an amused-looking Tay. "Do you need me to stay…?"

"No," Taliana says quickly. "I mean…" She cringes. "Never mind."

"He won't be far," Tay murmurs before I figure out how to respond. "In fact, he can stand guard right outside the door if you prefer."

I cut my best friend a look.

"It's his job as your guardian to do whatever you want," she goes on, clearly having fun with this designation now. "Like your own personal pet dragon."

My jaw threatens to tick again.

"Oh, he… he doesn't need to… I mean…" The little Omega growls, and it's the cutest sound I've ever fucking heard. "It's fine. *I'm* fine."

My irritation with Tay referring to me as a *pet dragon* melts away into amusement as I start weaving magic between my fingertips again. Only, instead of a standard coin, I find myself creating something a little more unique.

Taliana closes her eyes and inhales deeply again, a shudder rolling through her. It makes me wonder if she's as affected by my scent as I am by hers or if I'm imagining her relaxing movements.

Regardless, I feel the need to show my affection. A strange reaction, but one I embrace, as it's a need driven by my dragon's instincts.

As soon as the charm is ready, I return to Taliana's side to hold it out for her. "Here," I tell her. "Wear this, and if you need me, just touch the coin and it'll summon me to your side."

Just like a pet dragon, I think.

I'm certain Tay has a similar thought because she coughs to cover a laugh behind me.

Taliana glances down at the necklace I've created for her, the gold glistening with my magic. "Oh, this is… You don't have to…"

"I do," I insist, unclasping the item and holding it out for her. "May I?"

She's still staring at it, her beast back in her gaze as she —or rather, *they*—evaluates the gift.

I try not to think too much about what this means. Drakonians only craft gifts like this when they're trying to win favor from another Drakonian.

Or trying to entice a potential mate.

I've never created something like this for anyone. And especially not an Omega.

Fortunately, Taliana nods, thereby saving me from analyzing what this means. Or evaluating how and why I've suddenly lost my mind.

"Can you lift your hair for me?" I ask, admiring the long silver-black strands. My brother referred to it as a *waterfall* earlier. He wasn't wrong. It's shimmery like liquid and falls past her breasts.

Breasts I'm suddenly drawn to because they jut out as Taliana's hands move to do what I asked.

Tay clears her throat again behind me, propelling me into action.

Taliana's gaze holds mine as I clasp the chain against the back of her neck, the magic instantly sealing itself so only I can remove it. Is it possessive on my part? Yes. But I want her to wear my mark. It serves as a token of protection, one that will be respected by everyone in Gold Sector.

And all the other Drakon-Clan sectors, too.

If she asks me to take it off, I will.

But hopefully she'll accept the gift and display it for all to see.

My fingers linger against her skin, my thumb gently tracing the column of her throat before I force myself to move away from her.

I meant to tell Tay to evaluate Taliana for magical enchantments. However, other items came first. Fortunately, Tay is good at her job.

And the suspicious way she's looking between us now makes it clear that she's going to be exceptionally thorough in her exam.

"Remember, touch the charm and I'll return. Otherwise, I'll see you later in my suite." I turn to leave but catch Tay's shocked expression as I go. "You don't mind escorting her up there, right?" I ask her. "Or should I ask Onyx?"

My best friend swallows, her surprise amusing me greatly.

We didn't discuss this part, but I assumed it was a given considering I wanted to be the Omega's guardian. Typically, they stay in an Alpha's quarters for protection purposes. Not for knotting or sex or anything of the sort, just as a way to demonstrate good will and earn the Omega's trust.

It would be no different for Taliana.

Oh, she could share a room with her father. And maybe she should.

But I want to know everything about this Omega.

I also want to be the one who introduces her to Gold Sector culture.

"I'll escort her," Tay tells me after a beat.

"Thank you," I reply. "See you soon, Taliana."

I ash out of the room, not bothering at all to use the door, and take myself directly to the floor Taliana's father should be on. His guest room is really more like a cell, the magic in this area of the palace meant to hold visitors who haven't earned our trust yet.

He can technically leave, but he'll be monitored. Heavily.

And as a fellow Drakonian, he'll feel the weight of that monitoring with every step.

Which is why I'm not at all surprised to find him inside his room, seated by a small window that overlooks the ocean.

He didn't even bother closing the door, aware that there would be no privacy here. Or perhaps he was expecting this.

"Your Majesty," he murmurs without looking at me.

Well, it seems he recognizes me.

"It's fascinating that you address me formally, yet your daughter did not do the same," I say, stepping into his room and shutting the door behind me. "So let's chat, Alpha Keegan. You can start by telling me exactly what kind of hybrid your daughter is, then explain why she expected me to rape her with my knot."

CHAPTER FIVE
TALIANA

DOCTOR TAYLOR HAS LARGE EYES, THE COLOR OF OBSIDIAN stone.

Which, unfortunately, reminds me of my origin.

The black caves carved into the mountainside.

Inky-sand-covered beaches.

Opaque waters.

Shadowy beasts.

"Thirty more seconds," Doctor Taylor says as she studies the tablet in her hand. She ran it over me a few minutes ago after explaining that it would scan me for any internal injuries.

I'm not sure of the purpose, given my immortality, but I don't question her methods.

"Do you want to know how it works?" she asks, like she can read my mind.

"I… I don't really see the point," I admit, swallowing. "I don't get sick, and any injuries I've sustained have all healed already."

Doctor Taylor glances up with a frown. "I meant about the coin Oros gave you," she tells me. "But the scanner

39

isn't looking for injuries or illnesses so much as evidence of mistreatment."

My brow wrinkles. "Evidence of mistreatment?"

She nods as the device beeps. "Yes. Such as being fed suppressants to stall a heat." She arches a brow at me and tilts the screen toward me. "You're maybe a week away from going into estrus, and it's going to be quite painful as a result of suppressing your previous cycles."

I gape at the screen depicting basically every detail about my existence.

Hybrid Mix.

Drakonian markers present: 58.7%

X-Clan markers present: 37.6%

V-Clan markers present: 5.4%

W-Clan markers present: 0.1%

Superhybrid markers present: 0.9%

Estimated age: 21.54 Years

Last Estrus: Unknown

Next Estrus: Imminent

Suppressant Indicator: Positive

Stimulator Indicator: Negative

Knot Indicator: Negative

The list of *indicators* trails down the screen, suggesting it's an extensive list. "What's a, uh, stimulator indicator?" I ask, trying to ignore the glaring marks on my record that prove I'm part wolf and that I've taken suppressants.

"Stimulants force an Omega into heat. They're common in a lot of sectors and illegal here."

"So if an Omega is positive for one...?" I trail off, hoping she'll tell me in clear terms what's going to happen to me now that they know the truth about my history.

"Then the Omega will be given treatment," she answers without hesitation. "That's the point of this evaluation—to determine if an Omega requires medical attention. In your case, knowing that you've suppressed your heat for the last few years means we need to prioritize your comfort for your first cycle."

I stare at her. "Prioritize… my comfort?"

"Yes. You're going to need a knot."

Right. Hence the reason I'm here for a mate.

But I don't get a chance to add that part out loud because she's still speaking.

"You can either pick an Alpha for your nest, or we can introduce you to knot simulators. They're not exactly the same, but they'll help you through the worst of it."

Knot stimulator? I nearly ask.

Except she's still talking.

"Alternatively, we have some Omegas who choose to sleep through their estrus. I wouldn't recommend that in this case, as your cycle has already been significantly impacted, but we can discuss that option more if you prefer it."

I… I just gape at her. "I took suppressants."

"Yes. Were you unaware?" she asks, turning the screen back toward her and glancing down to type something.

"I… no. I mean, yes. I was aware. I willingly took them."

She nods. "Wise move to avoid hungry Alphas." She glances back up. "I apologize, but I missed some of the important intake questions. Which sector or area are you from?"

"Obsidian Sector," I tell her slowly, still confused as to why she's not reacting angrily to my suppressant information. *Is it because she's a Beta?*

"You had access to suppressants in Obsidian Sector?" she asks, finally showing a hint of surprise.

"No. Not exactly." I pinch my lips, trying to figure out how best to explain this. "My father worked for border patrol. He stole some from a contraband stash before we fled to the nomad lands. I think he hoped we would find more, but we never did. So I… I ran out recently."

"Which led you here," she finishes for me, nodding again. "We do have suppressants for extreme cases, but I can't in good conscience recommend them for you. You need to experience a few heats to regulate your cycle, or your dragon…" She glances at her tablet again. "Well, your dragon *or* your wolf, whichever you have, could be at risk of disassociating."

She starts scrolling on the screen—or I assume that's what her thumb is doing.

"When was your last shift?" she asks, her brow furrowing.

"Um, last week? Maybe two weeks ago?" I've lost track of time with all the traveling, hiding, and foraging. "Possibly three? I… I don't know."

She frowns at me. "You should shift before your cycle hits. But it may also cause you to go into estrus. So… I suggest you wait until your comfort plan is in place."

"I… Okay. But I haven't even been accepted yet? Or given permission to stay?"

She looks at my neck and then back up at my face. "That token around your neck suggests otherwise."

My brow furrows. "What do you mean?"

She considers me for a moment, then sets the tablet aside. "I think we should have that talk about Gold Sector now and the Omega relocation program."

"Uh, all right."

She reaches forward to tug on the cloak at my lap, but rather than pull it away, she draws it up. "You don't need to be naked for this."

"Oh." I kind of forgot all about my nude state. Stripping was normal for shifters. My nerves before were about being knotted. Then Oros made it clear that wasn't on today's agenda, so I stopped being concerned about my wardrobe. "Do you want me to get dressed?"

She shrugs. "I just want you to be comfortable, Taliana."

"I'm… comfortable."

Her lips twitch. "You're not, but that's okay. Most Omegas are extremely uncomfortable when they get here. Your situation is a little unique, as usually my patients are rescue cases, and I don't necessarily get that vibe from you. But I think you'll benefit from a thorough explanation."

She begins to pace.

Then she pauses and clears her throat, like she's ready to embark on a lecture. "Let's start from the beginning…"

CHAPTER SIX
OROS

"Your daughter is ashamed of her wolf?" I ask, repeating what Keegan just told me.

He also explained that she's a dragon-wolf hybrid but can only shift into her wolf half. And apparently, that upsets her.

"Taliana grew up in Obsidian Sector," he says by way of explanation. "They favor dragon genetics there. Everyone else is shunned."

"Then perhaps they should consider focusing on dragon procreation and cease all their hybrid experimentation," I say as I collapse into the chair seated across from him.

Surprise flickers across his oval-shaped face.

"Oh, don't give me that look," I tell him. "Of course I know what's happening in Obsidian Sector. Fuck, most of Drakon-Clan kind is aware that they're trying to create superior species. It's not the secret they think it is."

His features return to a state of uncertainty, his guarded expression causing his square jaw to flex.

"Why were you in Obsidian Sector?" I wonder aloud.

"Do you approve of their breeding program?" If he says yes, I'll escort him right off my island.

And I'll keep his daughter as payment for wasting my time.

Keegan leans forward to refill his glass with some fire ale, the bottle one I had delivered after he bluntly said, "Taliana anticipates the worst in Alpha kind because that's all she's ever known."

That was his response to my question about why his daughter thought I intended to rape her with my knot.

It was the exhaustion in his voice that had me calling for the drink. He clearly needed it.

But now I'm wondering why the fuck he was in Obsidian Sector in the first place.

He takes a long drink before setting the crystal glass down. "I went there for an Omega."

My eyebrow cocks upward. "You like them obedient and slave-like, then?"

His dragon growls deep, causing mine to stir in warning. "*No*. Fuck, I'm not a monster. If I were, I wouldn't be here trying to ensure that my daughter makes a decent match."

"You brought her here to make any match," I remind him. "There's no guarantee it'll be decent."

He gives me a long look, his irises flaring with a blend of black, silver, and white. "You've heard things about Obsidian Sector, and I've heard things about Gold Sector."

"That we like trading for Omegas, yes?"

"That you *care* for Omegas," he corrects me. "Riordan is an old friend."

My gaze narrows. "Then why didn't you take your daughter to him?"

"Because he suggested I come here instead. And…"

He blows out a breath and palms the back of his neck. "I need gold."

"So you want to sell your daughter," I translate, disgusted by the concept.

"No, I want her protected. I'll work for the gold." His hand falls from his neck to the arm of the charcoal-coated chair. "Taliana's safety is my priority. But I'm hoping, in time, I can visit and maybe work."

I study him. "Doing what?"

"I'm skilled at raiding," he tells me quietly. "I also know the Southern European nomad lands well, and I can suggest some camps you might be interested in raiding, too."

"I see." I fold my arms across my chest, ignoring the drinks on the small table between us. "So you went to Obsidian Sector for an Omega. Did you not know about their penchant for experimentation?"

"Oh, I had heard the rumors. I just didn't realize how true they were." He grabs his drink again and downs it, a haunted shadow overtaking his features.

He doesn't look a day older than me, our immortal genetics freezing our features around thirty years of age, sometimes younger. Yet his eyes hold a world of experience that somehow makes him appear decades older.

This male has lived through hell. It shows in the frown lines etched into his forehead. I wonder if he's ever truly smiled.

"I grew up with Riordan in Jasper Sector. We were lieutenants together for decades before the Infection, then led different camps in the new era. I specialized in raiding. He specialized in defense."

"Again leading me to wonder why you came to me and not him," I drawl.

"I'm getting there," he tells me, his words impatient,

yet his tone is interestingly respectful. "On a raid just over twenty years ago, I found an injured Omega lying in a nest."

His eyes close like he's picturing her now, his throat working to swallow.

"Her scent was unlike any other I'd ever sensed. I was instantly drawn to her. And she seemed to feel the same for me." His eyes open again, but rather than look at me, he focuses on the sea outside the window.

It's probably a good thing, as it gives me time to mask my reaction to what he just said. Because I understood that part a little too well, given my recent reaction to his daughter.

A sensation of unease stirs inside me, one that worsens as he continues.

"She went into heat and asked me to knot her. Naturally, I did. And I claimed her, too. I thought she was my mate. Just as I thought she felt the same way."

Yeah, that pit of unease is definitely worsening.

"She didn't," he goes on. "Or maybe she did. I don't know. But she left for Obsidian Sector, and I followed her. I thought I could convince her to return to Jasper Sector. However, her brainwashing became apparent quickly, and I was left with a choice—leave my chosen mate and our child, or try to fight for them."

He finally looks at me again. "You tried to fight."

"No. The moment I arrived in Obsidian Sector with her, I knew a fight would end in my death. So I opted for a third plan—to defect to Obsidian Sector, play their game, and quietly try to convince Helena to run away with me."

Despite everything, I find myself leaning forward. "And?"

"And that's when it became clear that Helena would never mate me." He pauses to refill his glass again.

Using a tablet on the table, I call for another bottle of ale, as well as some food, and wait for him to go on.

"Her scent was manufactured to attract the strongest compatible mate. She was put in that nest to lure me and trap me. And I wasn't the first, nor was I the last."

My jaw clenches. "Did your daughter inherit this trait?"

He stares at me. "You tell me. Is her scent alluring, Your Majesty?"

I don't answer him.

He nods. "Then I suppose it is." He sounds sad, not pleased. His scent doesn't smell sour, either, suggesting he's being truthful.

But I've met expert liars before.

And I don't trust this Drakon.

Not yet.

"How long did you stay in Obsidian Sector?"

"For seventeen years," he replies. "I traded my raiding expertise for the privilege of raising my daughter. It was that or let her grow up in a lab. But I knew they would come for her eventually. So I used my connections on the raids to gather as many suppressants as I could, then I made a decision no Alpha should ever have to make."

That haunted shadow ghosts across his features once more.

"I chose my daughter's fate over my mate." His jaw flexes, his hand clenching into a fist against the table. "I don't regret it. Taliana is an innocent in all this. And I kept her safe for as long as I could. But it's time. She needs a safe haven."

His gaze meets mine, a hint of a plea lurking in the multicolored depths.

"Please don't punish my daughter for things she can't control. If she smells alluring to you, it's because you're an ideal mate. She doesn't even know she possesses that talent. She also grew up hiding her wolf because she had to."

My teeth grind together at the thought.

No one should be ashamed of their beast.

We're shifters. Some more superior than others in terms of the food chain and magical abilities. But our animals are our spirits.

To suppress one's soul…

I nearly shake my head. I don't even want to think about the pain I would experience trying to *hide* my dragon.

"I hope what Riordan told me about Gold Sector is true," Keegan says. "I also hope that you'll accept my daughter for who she is. But if you can't do that, if you're going to punish her for a fate she never had a say in, then tell me now so I can take her away."

Possessive energy swirls around him, his dragon staring right at me through his eyes.

Well, one thing is very clear. This Alpha cares deeply about his daughter.

He may desire a payment for his trade, but I believe him when he says he wants a safe match for his daughter.

The other items will either be proved or disproved with Taliana's exam.

"I'll be in touch," I tell him, standing just as someone knocks on the door. "Enjoy your dinner. I ordered some of my favorite dishes for you."

It's not a lie.

He may not be an ally. But he's not an enemy yet, either.

"Thank you for meeting with me," Keegan says. "I appreciate the honor of your time, Your Majesty."

I dip my chin in acknowledgment.

Then ash upstairs to my office, hoping that maybe Onyx is still talking to Riordan.

Because I have some questions.

And I want to know more about that enchanting scent, I think. Riordan is the expert on all things Obsidian Sector. I've never questioned why that is.

But now I'm wondering if that expertise came from having a Drakon on the inside.

A Drakon named Keegan...

CHAPTER SEVEN
TALIANA

OMEGA RELOCATION PROGRAM.

The concept rolls through my mind as Doctor Taylor, who told me to call her Taylor, presses a series of buttons in the elevator.

"Hope you don't mind heights," she says. "We're going way up."

I don't reply. But I already knew we were traveling upward because of the fluttering in my belly.

I've longed to fly my whole life, my desire to soar in the clouds one I've dreamt of countless times.

Alas, my wolf can only fly across the ground on four paws.

Oh, I can run fast—a skill that has saved me more than once—but it lacks the freedom of gliding through the sky.

"We're at the tallest point on the island up here," she tells me as the doors open. "About nineteen hundred feet above sea level." She steps into the foyer of a residence. "Oros owns the entire floor."

I frown. "So he's important, then." Not a question, but

a comment. Because a dragon with superior quarters is a dragon with power.

"Yes. He's high-ranking."

"Is that normal for a guardian?" I ask as I glance around the open space. A large balcony decorates my right, the windowless wall granting full access. *For a dragon to enter*, I realize, noting the massive size.

A look to my left shows a similar entry.

Is the entire floor open like this? I wonder, glancing up at the white ceiling way above my head. *Yeah. Definitely built for a dragon.*

The elevator isn't big enough to hold one, but dragons would never want to be contained by a metal box.

"Normal? No." Her eyes sparkle like she knows something I don't.

Not surprising, given the circumstances.

She shared a lot with me about Gold Sector, though. Specifically about how Omegas are treated here.

"We assign a guardian to each one, always an Alpha, to help the Omega acclimate and learn to trust. The guardian's job is to protect you, but also introduce you to our way of life here. And there are absolutely no expectations involved in terms of mating, knotting, or anything else."

I questioned that last bit when she said it, and she went on to explain that her mate is an Omega.

Sheila, she told me.

A female Omega.

With a female Beta.

I didn't know that was possible. The Alphas of Obsidian Sector would never allow such a thing. Not necessarily the female-female aspect, but the Beta-Omega pairing.

Omegas are meant for Alphas and Alphas only.

Or that's what I was raised to believe.

But Taylor proved that isn't the case here. She even showed me a photo of her with her mate, the two of them smiling happily at a nearby beach.

"I can bring her by to meet you at some point," she offered before leading me up to Oros's suite. "If you're interested."

I didn't agree or disagree, just nodded and said I would let her know.

Because I wasn't sure what to think. I'm still not sure.

This is all so… unexpected.

Especially Oros's quarters. "It's beautiful up here," I whisper, admiring the view to my left. The ocean glitters in the distance as the sun begins to fall, the orange and red colors appealing to my inner wolf.

Above, I spy at least six dragons, all taking in the sights and stretching their wings.

Or maybe they're patrolling.

Regardless of their reasons for flying, it's a stunning display of power and Drakonian grace.

Is Oros among them? I wonder, my fingers finding his gold coin on instinct.

I thumb the metal, causing energy to spin around my fingertips. It's a welcome warmth that I rather like. "How does it work?" I ask Taylor, recalling her question from what felt like hours ago. "The coin, I mean."

She glances at my neck and then up at me. "You hold it like that and say his name out loud three times. Want to try it?"

"Oh, no," I say, dropping my hand instantly.

A devious grin splits across her lips. "Too bad. I would have enjoyed goading him a bit more." She glances around. "Well, make yourself at home. I'm sure Rumpel will be back soon."

My brow furrows. "Rumpel?"

"A nickname," she explains, smiling at me once more. "Oros is an old friend. He'll make a good guardian. But remember what I said—if you prefer a different Alpha, or a female, just let me know and I'll work on a match."

The serious quality in her tone from before and now tells me she means that. "Thank you," I reply. "I think I'll be okay with Oros, though." He seems nice enough.

And his scent is mouthwateringly addictive.

I can smell him everywhere here, despite the open air, and I very much want to stay.

"I think you'll be more than okay," she informs me softly, her eyes grinning now. "I'll send up some of the clothes we talked about, as well as some food and water. And don't forget what I said about shifting."

"No shifting yet," I echo, recalling the five times she stated those three words earlier.

"Excellent," she murmurs. "Need anything else before I work on the clothing bit?"

I glance around again. "Um, no. I should be okay... Oros really won't mind me waiting up here for him?"

She shrugs. "He said to escort you here."

That's true; I heard him say that, too. "Okay." I guess that means... I can wander? Explore? Maybe just... look at the view?

"Make yourself at home, Taliana," she tells me. "Take a shower or a bath. Grab some water from his en-suite kitchen. Do whatever you need to feel comfortable. Trust me, he won't mind."

My lips twist, but I nod and repeat, "Okay." Taylor claimed they were friends. So... so she must know what he'll be fine with and what he won't like, right? "Thank you for your guidance, and, um, everything."

For not judging me for taking suppressants.

For not judging me for having a wolf.
For not judging me for, well, everything.

I didn't add any of those items aloud, though. Primarily because I have no way of knowing if she truly judges me or not. But she doesn't seem to.

In fact, she said I wasn't the only one without a dragon on the island.

But she never elaborated on what that meant or where they might be.

Maybe Oros will tell me.

"If you need anything else, just touch the screen here. It'll call up an operator for you." She gestures to the all-white wall, making my eyes narrow until she presses her palm to the center. Then my eyes widen as the cement-like texture transforms into a touch screen.

"Wow," I breathe. "Does that happen on every wall?"

"No, only the ones with markings." She flicks her wrists to cause the technology to disappear once more, then points to a raised white stone. "These, see?"

"Oh." Yeah, I see it… sort of. It's barely visible.

"You'll start to notice them, but a trick is to look near elevator bays like this one." She moves toward said elevator while speaking and clicks the button beside it—that one I can see because it's framed by gold metal. "I'll be back to check on you tomorrow."

"Okay. Um, thank you again."

"Anytime." With another of her friendly grins, she gives me a wave and ducks into the elevator as soon as it opens, leaving me alone in Oros's suite.

I stand there for a moment, then decide to "make myself at home" like she suggested and give myself a tour.

———

Thirty minutes later, a few things are clear to me.

First, this suite has no windows and barely any exterior walls.

Second, gold is the decorative metal of choice.

Third, there's only one bed.

Oh, it's a massive bed, one clearly designed for a dragon. Which means sharing it isn't impossible.

Except my wolf is already begging me to *nest*.

I can't remember the last time I experienced this urge. Maybe before taking my suppressants? When I nearly went into my first heat?

Regardless, it's hitting me hard now.

Hence the reason I'm currently standing next to the giant bed, holding a pillow.

A pillow that smells like an autumn campfire. *Smoky sensuality. Warmth on a cold night. A blissful—*

The clearing of a throat has me whirling around and meeting the gaze of an Alpha with vibrant silver eyes.

He arches a silver-white brow as I continue to gape at him. "Erm." I clear my throat. "Hi?"

"Hi?" he repeats, and his familiar voice sends frost through my veins.

Because it's him. *Voice.*

The Prince of Gold Sector.

I fall into an awkward curtsy, my focus instantly dropping to the floor. "Your Majesty, please forgive me."

His resulting silence sends a shiver through me.

Why is he here? Did he see my evaluation results? Is he here to punish me for taking suppressants? Ridicule me for having a wolf?

"You know, it's quite rude to explore spaces that don't belong to you," he tells me.

I swallow, my heart suddenly in my throat. "I'm sorry, Your Majesty." I don't even try to explain that Taylor said this would be okay. Maybe she set me up. Or maybe she thought it would be fine.

Regardless, I'll own my mistake.

Because deep down, I knew better.

This is an Alpha's sanctuary. Not mine.

"Hmm," Voice hums. "Why are you here, Omega?"

"Alpha Oros instructed Doctor Taylor to bring me to his suite after my evaluation," I inform him, my gaze still on the ground as I remain in my reverent position.

Although, I'm not sure how much longer I can curtsy like this, as my legs are beginning to tremble from the effort.

"Did he?" I can't tell, but he almost sounds amused. It must be my imagination because there's no way he could possibly be amused by me.

"Yes," I confirm, unsure of what else to say.

"Taliana," he murmurs, his warmth bleeding into me as he moves to stand right in front of me. "Please stop bowing."

I bite my cheek and slowly stand, my legs wobbly as I do. "I'm sorry, Your Majesty."

"And stop…" He trails off. "Stop apologizing."

"I…" I almost repeat myself but cease speaking.

He sighs, and the sound makes me shudder. I've heard that disappointing huff many times in my life, and the aftermath is never pleasant. "This is… unexpected. But I suppose we'll see if you're worthy soon."

Does that mean he hasn't seen my evaluation results yet? I wonder, unsure of what to say next. *Or is there going to be another trial of some kind?*

"Try to stay out of trouble, Omega," he adds. "And remember to respect your accommodations. This isn't a typical guest suite, but an Alpha's quarters. All right?"

I nod. "Yes, Your Majesty. I apologize for any disrespect I've shown you or Alpha Oros."

He's quiet again, but I can still see his silver shoes. They're a stark contrast to my bare feet. At least I changed back into my old dress before venturing up here. Standing naked before him would be too much. But I'm sure I appear dirty and cheap in this opulent suite.

No wonder he doesn't want me to wander.

He's probably afraid I'll soil everything I touch.

"Hmm," he hums again, taking a step back. "Nice necklace, Omega. Tell me, do you have any idea what it means?"

I lift my fingers to touch the gold coin. "It allows me to call for Oros."

"Is that what he told you?"

My brow furrows. "Yes, Your Majesty."

"Nothing else?"

I recall everything Oros said and shake my head. "No, Your Majesty."

More silence.

"Gold is a coveted metal in Gold Sector," he finally says, his tone holding a note of reverence. "I suggest you not only wear that necklace to your next audience with the court but also bring any other gifts you're given. The more items you can present, the better you'll be received. Do you understand?"

My lips nearly curl down.

Do I understand? Yes. In theory, anyway.

Oros's gold necklace must be a symbol of protection, or maybe affection, or both. And the Gold Sector Prince is saying these symbols will help me gain favor with the court.

Perhaps even enough to overlook my flaws, to overlook my *wolf*.

Gingerly, I dip my chin. "Yes, Your Majesty."

"Good." He steps back, his silver shoes disappearing from my view. "Enjoy your time here, Omega. But remember what I said—respect your accommodations. You have no idea how unique or important this opportunity is for you."

I nod again. "Thank you, Your Majesty."

He doesn't reply, doesn't make a sound at all.

I wait, listening for his footsteps, but hear nothing. Not even with my enhanced hearing.

Only, I can sense that he's left because his scent—one that reminds me of a harsh spice—dissipates entirely. And all I can smell in his wake is that soothing aroma of a simmering campfire.

Oros, I think, inhaling deeply.

The urge to nest hits me hard again.

But I don't dare ponder his bed any longer. Rather, I lift my gaze tentatively to confirm that the Gold Sector Prince has left, then force my feet to move back to the foyer.

This isn't my space.

Which means I should wait for Oros by the elevators.

I could stroke the coin and say his name three times to call for him, but I don't want to bother him.

Instead, I simply stand, head bowed, and strive for patience.

I can do this.
I will do this.
I have to do this.

CHAPTER EIGHT
OROS

"Did you or did you not instruct me to question Alpha Keegan?" my brother asks as he steps into my office.

I don't look up from the screen I was reading when he entered and simply reply, "I changed my mind."

"Clearly," he drawls. "Just like you changed your mind about the Omega's accommodations?"

Now that grabs my attention and forces me to focus on my brother.

Which leads me to narrowing my gaze. "I'm not sure I like the judgment in your expression right now, Onyx."

"Well, I'm not sure I like the judgment—or lack thereof —you're using where that Omega is concerned, brother."

My jaw ticks. "Why are you riding my tail?"

"Because you seem to have handed the reins to your knot," he tosses back.

"Oh, fuck off, Onyx," I mutter, returning my attention to the screen before me.

He chuckles in response. "My, but that pretty little Omega has your beast in a twist, and you just met."

I ignore him, instead focusing on the message I'd started drafting before he interrupted me. It doesn't matter that I originally came up here in hopes of finding him. He can wait until I'm ready to speak now.

It seems your pet spy is in my sector, I type. *His meeting with the court occurred right before your call with my brother, too. And you know how I feel about coincidences, Rio. If you feel this strongly about trade routes, perhaps we should arrange a flight so we can discuss things properly? Dragon to dragon.*

I read over my message as my brother collapses onto the couch positioned across from my desk. He's thankfully remained quiet since his little quip about my beast.

Satisfied with my missive, I hit Send and let the words fly across the Mediterranean Sea to former-day Majorca.

Riordan may own all the islands south of Spain, but I own the Greek Isles.

Obsidian Sector is the one in between, taking over Sicily and Malta.

Not that any of those past names still apply.

But we're all old enough to remember them anyway.

"By the way," my brother drawls. "Your Omega thinks I'm the Gold Sector Prince."

That seizes my attention. "You went to see her?" I ask, closing my screen.

"I went to see you and found her instead," he replies.

Shit. "Did you correct her?"

"No."

I frown. "Why not?"

"She's yours," he says simply as he sets his ankle over his opposite knee. "I may not agree with that decision, but I still respect it. So that makes it not my place to correct her, but yours."

I study him for a moment, considering my options. I've

purposely not told her who I am, mostly as a means to keep her calm. I want her to confide in me. To *trust* me.

And that'll be hard to do if she knows my title.

Being Prince of Gold Sector isn't who I am, though. I'm still just Oros.

"I'll think about how to handle that situation," I tell my brother. "Thank you for not correcting her."

His chin angles downward in acknowledgment. "There's something I don't understand, though."

"Only one thing?" I ask.

He grunts. "Okay, several things. But at the top of my list is how her father could bring her here and not give her your name."

I consider that for a long moment. "I'm not sure. However, he knew me when I went to visit."

"Of course he did. So why not share your identity with his daughter?"

I shake my head. "Not a fucking clue. Maybe you should go ask him."

"You know, I would, but the last time you gave me a task, you went and did it yourself. So I think I'll leave this one for you to do."

I roll my eyes. "I went to him to figure out why his daughter thought I was going to rape her."

His eyebrow arches. "And?"

"He basically told me her upbringing in Obsidian Sector preprogrammed her to believe certain things about Alphas." Rather than wait for my brother's comments on that topic, I proceed to tell him everything else Keegan said, including the details about Riordan. "You walked in as I was sending Rio an email. I assume he didn't mention anything to you during your call with him?"

My brother grunts. "Our call ended shortly after he realized you weren't coming."

I sigh. "Who ended it?"

Onyx smiles. "I did."

"Of course you did."

"He said, and I quote, 'I have no interest in meeting with Gold Sector's second-in-command.'" He shrugs again. "I'm not one to beg for an audience, so I told him to have a good day, then, and hung up."

"Have a good day?" I parrot.

"Well, it may not have been that polite. But the point was the same." He unhooks his ankle from his knee to set his silver-coated boot on the ground and leans forward with his forearms on his thighs. "Do you believe Keegan? About why he's here?"

"Yes and no," I murmur. "I'm waiting for Taylor's evaluation file to confirm the facts."

"I doubt he lied about her being a wolf."

"It would be a poor decision on his part," I say, agreeing with my brother's assessment. "Same with the information on the suppressants."

He nods, then gives me a thoughtful look. "You gave her a token of favor."

"I did."

His light-colored eyebrow arches upward. "Before or after you learned about her wolf?"

"Before."

"And now?" he presses.

"And now…" I repeat, drawing out the answer. "And now, I don't know. Not because of her wolf, but because of her scent." I already told him what Keegan said about Taliana's mother and how she laid a trap for him. "It could be a trap."

"Indeed," he agrees, his lips curling down. "But she doesn't smell unique to me at all."

"Then you're not the one being ensnared."

"You said Keegan claimed it only works on compatible mates, right?"

"Yes."

"Then…" He waves a hand.

"Then what?" I ask, not following his train of thought.

"You're compatible." He utters the words like that should be obvious.

It is, but why he's pointing it out is less clear.

"And?" I prompt him.

"And nothing. You're compatible. Full stop." He lifts a shoulder in another of his trademark shrugs. "Unless she's been programmed to also ensnare you, I don't see the issue. If anything, the scent thing just makes it easier to identify an ideal mate. That takes some of the guesswork out of the equation. Doesn't seem so bad to me."

I frown at him. "Unless it's all founded on a lie."

"But it's not. Keegan said it was designed to attract compatible mates. Nothing wrong with that unless you intend to abuse the outcome. So I guess the real question is, what are her intentions? Are they good or bad?"

"I don't know."

"Well, of course not. You just met. Yet she's exploring your suite because you gave her free rein to your personal space. Perhaps you should go check on that."

I wince. "There's not much she can do up there."

"Oh, I don't know. I found her by your bed when I entered."

My eyebrows shoot upward. "You did? Doing what?"

"Looked like she was considering the potential for a nest," he tells me, making me jump up with a curse.

"Why didn't you say something when you first arrived?" I demand.

He gives me one of his famous smiles—the one that

he's used for centuries when finding enjoyment at my expense. "Maybe I wanted to give her time to finish."

My fingers curl, the urge to deck him hitting me square in the chest.

But as I take a step around my desk toward him, I realize it's not the notion of Taliana nesting that bothers me. It's the knowledge that my brother was near her and her potential nest.

In my room.

Ice pours over me, freezing me mid-step.

Fuck.

This is bad.

I shouldn't want the Omega to nest in my room. But I... I do. And I want to be there when she does it.

"I need to go," I tell him, heading for the door. I'm almost through the threshold when the dinging of an elevator announces Taylor's arrival.

She steps out, a look of surprise crossing her features upon seeing me leaving my office.

"Is she a wolf?" I ask as I head straight for her.

Taylor doesn't ask me who I mean. "Yes."

"And she was on suppressants?" I add.

"Yes," she confirms. "She's never had a heat. I give her a week at most before her estrus hits, and it's going to be painful."

I nod and move around her to catch the elevator doors before they close. "Thank you, Tay." I don't have any other questions. She's told me enough to confirm Keegan's comments about Taliana.

The rest, I'll need to deduce for myself.

Either this is all a trap—one orchestrated by Rio or the asshole in charge of Obsidian Sector...

Or this is fate.

There's only one person who can show me the truth, and that's the Omega waiting in my suite.

All right, little diamond, I think, keying in the code for my floor. *Let's see who you really are and what this scent enchantment truly means...*

CHAPTER NINE

TALIANA

THE SCENT OF WARM BREAD TEASES MY NOSTRILS, MAKING me salivate. It arrived what feels like hours ago, but realistically, it's only been ten or fifteen minutes. I just can't remember the last time I ate.

Taylor sent it up with the clothes she'd promised.

But I don't dare touch any of it.

The Gold Sector Prince made himself very clear—this suite is not mine. Nothing here belongs to me. I need to respect that. *And ignore what Taylor said.*

Except… if she lied to me about making myself comfortable in Oros's suite, what else did she lie to me about?

I shiver, uncertain.

Where's my father? I wonder. *He would know what to do right now… who to trust.*

But he didn't prepare me for all these strange rules. For Oros's kindness.

Unless it's all a trick. A trial. A test…

My fingers twist before me, my nerves fluttering inside me. Or maybe that's my hunger.

Moons, I can almost taste the bread on my tongue. Except I probably can't swallow it in this state. My throat is too dry, my mouth—

Ding.

My limbs freeze, the sound indicating another arrival. *More food? More clothes? The Gold Sector Prince?*

But as the refreshing scent of campfire swirls around me, followed by a kiss of power, I know it's none of the above.

It's Oros.

I immediately look at him, needing to see his gold eyes, his familiar features, his *smile.*

However, he's not smiling as he enters. Instead, he's frowning.

Shit. The prince must have told him about my snooping. "I'm sorry for exploring your personal space," I blurt out, instinctively dropping my gaze. "It was disrespectful of me, and I apologize. Please forgive me."

Please still be my guardian, I want to add. But that just sounds pathetic.

Of course, I feel pathetic right now. And alone. *So very alone.*

"What?"

Crap. I must not have explained myself well. "I… I didn't mean to intrude on your quarters. I should have…" Well, I don't know what I should have done. "Stayed here?" It comes out like a question because I really have no idea what's expected of me.

And the confusion is starting to exhaust me.

"Taliana." There's a hint of command in his tone, one that has me looking at him on instinct. "I invited you into my quarters. You're free to treat them as your own."

I stare back at him, confused. "But the prince said…"

He arches a perfectly sculpted brow. "Finish that statement. What were you told?"

"He... he reminded me that these are your quarters and I should respect them."

"Well, he's not wrong. But that doesn't mean you can't make yourself at home." He steps toward me with a small smile. "You're safe here, Taliana. And I don't mind you treating my space as your own."

"Is that what guardians are required to do?"

"It's what they volunteer to do," he tells me.

"And... and we share everything?"

"We can share whatever you like."

"Including... the bed?" I ask, my cheeks suddenly warm. "To sleep, I mean. Not... not... the..." I close my eyes and growl a little, irritated with myself for stammering.

I grew up in an environment where this was required of me, but over the last few years, I've tasted freedom unlike any I've ever known.

And my father encouraged my independence.

Yet he told me to bow upon arriving here, to respect the Gold Sector Alphas, to win over a mate. But what's the point if it turns me into this incoherent mess?

"Your bed makes me want to nest," I grit out, too exhausted and overwhelmed to hide how I'm feeling. "I'm also really hungry and thirsty. And... and I *hate* this dress."

I finally open my eyes again and find him smiling at me, like he's amused.

"None of this is funny," I tell him, miffed at the humor dancing in his gaze. "I haven't slept well in weeks. I haven't eaten a meal in... Actually, I'm not sure how long. And the bath I took before arriving here today was in the ocean, so all I taste is salt."

He's no longer smiling.

Probably because I gave him a tone.

Which is the wrong thing to do with an Alpha.

But it's been a really long day. All I want is a bath, some food, and a nap.

In that very comfortable bed meant for nesting, I think, shivering.

"All right, *printesa mea*," he murmurs, the foreign words sounding hypnotic on his tongue. "Come with me."

He doesn't wait for me to obey, instead moving forward with purpose through the foyer. He only pauses to pick up a tray with one hand and a bag with the other, then continues into the living area of his suite.

I follow because what else am I going to do?

But as he bypasses the dining table—adjacent to his kitchen—and saunters through his bedroom, I begin to frown.

That frown deepens when he leads me into his opulent bathroom.

I freeze on the threshold as he sets the tray down near one of the sinks. The bag goes to the floor, and the Alpha faces me once more. "Come here," he beckons.

And for whatever reason, my feet do what he asks.

His lips curl a little, like he knows I'm no longer in control, and he catches my hips.

My breathing halts, my insides turning to liquid as I all but melt into his touch.

Except he doesn't pull me closer. He lifts me up onto the counter instead, situates me between the sinks, lets go…

And hands me a water bottle from the bag.

"Drink," he demands.

I blink dumbly at him for a full second before I do exactly as he says.

It's like I'm a puppet.

Yet I'm not sad about it. Actually, it's kind of nice having someone tell me what to do. Especially when the results of those commands make me feel good.

Within a minute of drinking water, I can already breathe a little easier. And as I finish the contents, the salty brine lingering in my mouth almost dissipates.

"Now eat this." He hands me a warm croissant stuffed with something savory.

Ham? I guess as the first bite hits my tongue. *Cheese, too.*

Gods, I can't remember the last time I ate something so decadent. So filling. So *tasty*.

Maybe my nineteenth birthday after my father caught a particularly large fish. He smoked it that night, the delicious flavor one I dreamt about for weeks after.

One of the upsides to being immortal is not needing food to survive.

But that doesn't mean one doesn't suffer from hunger.

I know from experience just how starved an immortal can feel. Which allows me to enjoy this meal even more.

I finish it faster than I should, only to be rewarded with a bowl of berries soon after.

Oros doesn't need to tell me what to do with them; I start indulging in the flavor before he can even speak. By the time I finish, he looks amused again.

I'm too content for that look to bother me now.

"Better?" he asks.

"Yes." It comes out on a sigh, one that seems to amuse him even more.

"Good." He places his palms on the marbled counter on either side of my hips. "Now I want you to strip."

My bubble of contentment pops. "Wh-what?"

"We are going to take a shower together. And I'm going to show you how Alphas treat Omegas in Gold Sector."

I swallow. "Oh. Um. Okay."

If he notices my discomfort, he doesn't comment on it. Instead, he rotates toward the large shower and turns on three different heads.

There are actually five in total, something I focus on as I try to calm my now-racing heart.

"Taliana," he says, his subtle accent curling around my name.

I look at him and notice that all his gold has vanished, leaving him shirtless in front of me.

He's very... sculpted.

Just like an Alpha should be.

Yet there's something even more majestic about this male. Maybe it's his scent. Or it might be the powerful aura surrounding him.

I'm not really sure. But whatever it is, it's alluring.

I find myself leaning toward him, only for his hands to suddenly snag my hips and drag me off the counter. My palms land on his bare chest, his skin hot against mine.

Every part of me shivers.

This is it. The knotting test. I'm sure of it.

Only, a strange thing happens. The expected sensation of dread never comes. Instead, I feel something else entirely.

A hint of unease, perhaps? The subtle churn deep inside?

Except it's not very unpleasant. It's... it's welcome. Warm. *Enticing.*

"If you prefer, I can keep my pants on," he tells me. "But most shifters don't mind nudity. So I just assumed..."

I nod. "It's... it's fine. But Doctor Taylor said I'm not allowed to shift." Something I'm eternally grateful for now because it means I have a reason not to reveal my wolf.

"Oh? Did she say why?" he asks, his hands still on my hips.

"Um, yes. She said it might cause me to go into heat. So she advised me not to shift until I have a plan in place for that." My cheeks burn with the admission.

Not only is it embarrassing, but it also somewhat links back to the suppressants.

And while Taylor didn't seem to think it was a big deal, I'm sure this Alpha would disagree. All Alphas would.

"Mmm, and did you discuss potential plans?" His voice lowers an octave with that question, his thumbs suddenly burning me through the thin fabric of my dress.

"We discussed options," I admit, my voice breathier than intended.

He nods. "Good." He draws a circle against my hip. "Alphas in Gold Sector respect an Omega's choice, Taliana. That's what I want to prove to you."

I stare up into his gold eyes. "Why?"

"Because consent matters here." He tugs on my dress. "Now, will you let me take care of you? Or would you prefer to shower alone?"

"I have a choice?"

A serious expression overcomes his handsome features, and he releases me. "Always."

"Okay." I study him for a beat. "I… I want to know what you mean by taking care of me. Show me."

Because I want to trust him. Even if I can't have him.

Once he realizes I'm a wolf, he probably won't want me.

But I want to experience what it's like to be a desirable Omega. A true Drakonian.

Oros says nothing, just reaches for me again. Except this time he takes hold of my dress and slowly draws it upward.

It's intimate.

Unexpected.

Arousing.

It's particularly erotic because he's holding my gaze the whole time. At least until the fabric moves over my head. But as he drops the garment to the ground, his focus is still on my face, his golden eyes swirling with heat. "Still okay?" he asks me.

I nod.

"Good. Now go stand under the water. I'll join you in a moment."

My feet move on autopilot, my body seeming to bend to his every command.

I'm not bothered by it, though. I rather like the relief I feel being under his control. Like I'm safe to just… exist. To simply *breathe*.

My wolf likes him. Perhaps a bit too much. Because there's no part of me that feels uneasy in his presence. It's all so natural. So *right*.

I barely feel the warm water on my skin or the slick tiles beneath my feet. I'm too focused on his movements behind me to appreciate that this is the first hot shower I've taken since living in Obsidian Sector.

His heat bathes my skin as he steps in right behind me, his scent a blanket of comfort to my senses.

Gods, I can't tell if it's my impending heat or him, but I… I haven't felt anything like this before.

Instant safety.

Deep need.

A bizarre desire to wrap myself up in his arms and stay there for eternity.

It's like my wolf is threatening to come out of my skin and rip right into him. Not to hurt him, but to… to bite him. To *claim* him.

Moons, this is bad.

This has to be my estrus. Taylor warned me it would be intense. But this…? I…

A purr ignites behind me as Oros takes hold of my hips and draws me back into him.

He's naked.

I can feel him. Every hard, muscular inch.

And it takes considerable effort not to rotate toward him, to bury my head in his rumbling chest, and explore him with my hands.

"Is this okay?" he asks me.

I can't speak, my tongue too thick for my mouth, so I nod instead. It's more than okay. It feels amazing to be touched like this. Held. *Protected.*

"Can I wash your hair?"

I nod again, swallowing as his fingertips gently run up my sides. One hand leaves, the other trailing all the way up before shifting back to round my shoulder and reach my neck. He pulls my hair aside and leans down, his lips against my ear. "You're a beautiful Omega, printesa mea," he whispers.

My eyes fall closed. "Thank you," I somehow manage to say, the words a bit choked. I don't think an Alpha has ever called me *beautiful* before.

"I bet your wolf is just as stunning," he adds, causing me to freeze against him.

My wolf.

He… he knows… about my wolf.

CHAPTER TEN

OROS

"Shh," I hush, my lips tasting her throat as her pulse beats rapidly in her neck. This isn't what I intended to do upon returning to my suite, but her apology did something to me.

Well, it did a few things.

First, it made me want to ash back to my office and punch my brother in the face—because *what the fuck* was he thinking lecturing her about my space?

But then I realized we needed to establish some trust between us.

Trust that I'll take care of her.

And trust… that she isn't here to betray me. Trust that she isn't a trap, like her mother was for her father.

It's possible that this is all some sort of ploy, her scent a beacon meant to tempt me into falling. However, when her head snapped up and she told me about her desire to nest, her exhaustion, her desire for something as simple as food and water, all hints of potential reservations vanished into smoke.

There's only one way to determine her motives now,

and that's to experience whatever this is between us. To embrace it. To show her who I am, and let her return the favor in kind.

That's why I mentioned her wolf—because her father warned me that she's ashamed of her inner beast. And I want her to know that I'm not.

Wolves are majestic. Fierce. Gorgeous in their own right.

"We worship all kinds of Omegas here," I tell her, my fingers drawing through her hair as my opposite hand slips around to palm her flat belly. "Let me prove it to you." I boldly kiss her neck, my dragon purring with approval inside.

He wants me to sink my canines into her and mark her. *Claim* her.

And I can't remember ever feeling such a powerful pull in my life.

It's like my soul has known hers for an eternity already.

Which is ridiculous.

But I'm not about to run away from this connection between us.

"Alpha dragons hate wolves," she whispers, the choked quality of her voice causing me to spin her around in my arms. Her eyes are filled with tears, her bottom lip trembling.

"Dragons do not hate wolves," I tell her. "And anyone who has fed you that lie doesn't deserve his knot."

She gazes up at me with such heartfelt agony that it hurts to fucking breathe.

Fires, this woman has been through hell. I can see the nightmares rolling through her gaze like flashes of violent thunderstorms. It sucks the air right out of the room.

How have I missed this pain? I ask myself, transfixed by her torment. It's so apparent in her features now that I wonder if I missed it before because I was too blinded by her beauty to see her true self. But I definitely see her now.

"Do you really think...?" She trails off, swallowing. "Will a Drakonian Alpha accept me?"

"Oh, *printesa mea*," I whisper, my forehead falling to hers. "There's no doubt in my mind that you'll be claimed."

And if I'm not careful, I'll be the one to do it.

It's expected that I'll one day take a mate, to produce an heir for Gold Sector.

That's a lot to ask of an Omega I've just met. Especially one with such a haunted past.

I also can't believe I'm even considering it. The expectation has always been there, but I've never been inclined to act on it.

Until now.

Until *her*.

Taliana clings to me, then nods. "Thank you."

My purr intensifies, the sound coming more from my dragon than from me. *Purring* is a sacred act, one reserved for an Alpha and his mate.

Yet it feels so natural to purr for her now.

I'm in so much fucking trouble, I realize. It's partly her scent. Or maybe even mainly her scent. But it's also *her*. This female. This enchanting Omega. *Printesa mea.*

It's an endearment I've never used with anyone else. *My princess.*

The words suit her perfectly.

Especially when she's fiery and telling me what she needs—like in the foyer of my suite.

I liked that side of her. And I want more.

However, I take a step back to continue showing her how Alphas treat Omegas here. That was the entire point of this exercise. Or that's what I told myself when I initially suggested it.

Again, not my plan at all.

However, here we are.

And I'm not mad about it.

She stares up at me with reverence as I grab the shampoo and begin lathering it into her silver-black hair. The color is darker from the water, almost resembling midnight strands spun with white gold. An intoxicating hue, one that contrasts beautifully with the yellow gold hanging from her neck.

My token sits perfectly between her breasts, the subtle claim pleasing me greatly.

Although, noting the expanse of naked skin beyond it has me wanting to decorate more of her in gold. *Hmm. An anklet, perhaps*, I think, considering the option briefly before returning my focus to her hair.

She's still staring at me like I've hung the moon for her, those alluring eyes fixated on mine as I run my fingers through her silky strands.

"Close your eyes," I tell her softly before guiding her under the water.

She follows my command beautifully, just like she's done all day. *The perfect Omega*, I think. *Feisty when she needs to be. Submissive when I need her to be.*

It takes significant effort not to kiss her.

She's not mine. Not yet. I just want to take care of her, something I've never truly desired to do before with anyone else. Oh, I've held Omegas. Stroked them. But this... this is on another level entirely.

I'm petting her. Conditioning her hair. *Washing* her.

When I pick up the soap—a bar that smells like me— I'm suddenly so hard I almost feel dizzy. Because *fuck*. I'm about to put my hands all over her. Drench her in my scent. *Make her…* mine.

Alarms blare in my head. Alarms I ignore in favor of touching her.

She shudders beneath my palms, goose bumps pebbling along her flesh. Fires, it makes me want to lick her. See if she tastes as good as she smells.

My nose goes to her hair as I step behind her, my hands roaming up and down her arms. She mentioned bathing in the sea before attending the meeting with the Royal Court earlier. But not once have I picked up that scent from her.

Just a fresh meadow. On a sunny day.

Fucking heaven.

I close my eyes, my nose burrowing deeper into her hair as I explore her sides, the soap slippery against her skin. Everything I do is on autopilot—switching the bar from palm to palm, lathering it in slow, hypnotic circles, ensuring every inch of her torso is covered.

Everything except her tits…

"Taliana," I breathe, my lips brushing her hair. "If I make you uncomfortable, say 'Rumpel' and I'll stop what I'm doing."

I can't think of a more jarring nickname. *Alpha* and *Your Highness* will probably have the opposite effect from her lips.

But *Rumpel* will definitely halt my actions.

As would *Rumpelstiltskin.* However, that's a mouthful.

"Isn't that… what Taylor calls you?" she asks slowly.

"Yes. Because of my brother." I pull back a little, my hands falling to her hips to guide her around to face me. "It's a name that will instantly ground me and force me to stop."

She frowns at me. "I don't understand."

If there was any doubt as to her innocence, it's gone now. Because I can see the confusion in her gaze. She has no idea what she's doing to me or what I want to do to her.

"I don't want to push your boundaries, Taliana," I explain. "I need you to trust me and be comfortable with me. Which means you have to tell me if I'm doing something you dislike. And if you can't formulate the words, just say 'Rumpel.'"

"Rumpel," she repeats. "Why do they call you that?"

It's not really relevant to our conversation, but it's a welcome distraction. Because I can feel myself losing control. Especially with her tits so close to my chest.

And her cunt inches from my aching knot.

"Rumpelstiltskin," I grate out.

Which naturally deepens her frown. "What?"

"It's a fairy tale."

"Okay…" She blinks at me.

"About an imp," I go on. "Once upon a time, a miller claimed his daughter could spin straw into gold. The king of their land found out, took the girl, and demanded that she prove it. Except it was all a lie."

"Why would he lie?"

"Fame," I suggest, glancing over her. "There are a lot of reasons people lie."

Or set traps, I think.

But I don't add that part out loud.

"Regardless, it was a lie. So an imp agrees to help her by spinning the straw into gold for her in exchange for her necklace. The king, naturally, is delighted at her proven talent and demands more. Thus, the imp helps again, this time for her ring. And the king declares that if she can do it a third time, he'll wed her."

"Because he believes her lie," Taliana says slowly.

"Exactly."

"Well, does she tell him the truth?" she presses, her gaze searching mine as though she's intrigued to know how this tale ends.

"No. She makes a deal with the imp instead."

"More jewelry in exchange for gold?" she guesses.

I shake my head. "When he returns to offer help, she says she has nothing else to trade. So he requests her firstborn instead."

Taliana gasps. "Oh, no. So then she tells the king the truth?"

I chuckle and shake my head again. "Of course not. She agrees to the exchange—her firstborn for more gold—so she can wed the king."

Taliana looks positively distraught. "*What?*"

Well, perhaps this discussion was a wise one to have after all. Because that was a telling response. "She chooses to become a queen, basically, over her firstborn," I say, shrugging like that doesn't bother me. When in reality, it very much does. "Which—"

"*How* could someone do that?" she interjects, her cheeks bright red with fury. "What a ridiculous choice. She should have just told the truth."

"The king might have killed her," I point out. "Or ousted her and her father, at a minimum."

"Both are preferable outcomes to giving up a child," she snaps, clearly furious. "What a horrible story."

I arch a brow. "I haven't even finished it yet."

"I don't think I want to know how it ends." She looks away, her face contorting into a cute little pout. "Actually, no. I need to know. Does she… keep her child? Or not have one?"

"Oh, she has one. And she immediately realizes how wrong she was to agree to the deal."

Taliana slowly returns her gaze to mine. "Okay. So… what does she do?"

"Makes another deal."

She rolls her eyes. "Of course she does."

"The imp gives her three chances to guess his name and says that if she gets it right, he'll forfeit the claim on the child."

Her gaze narrows. "And his name is Rumpel?"

"Rumpelstiltskin," I correct her.

"And she guesses that?" she asks, sounding shocked.

"No. Her first two tries are wrong. Then she follows him and overhears someone else say his name, so when he comes back for her third guess—"

"She cheats and gives the name," she finishes for me.

I nod.

"I see." Her brow furrows, like she's seriously considering the moral of the story. "I still don't like her."

A chuckle escapes me. "Yeah? Why?"

"Because she lied to the king, used the imp, and nearly gave up her child to become a queen. She's clearly not a good Omega."

"Well, I never said she was an Omega."

"Fine. She wasn't a good Alpha or Beta or shifter or whatever." She folds her arms over her breasts like she's completely forgotten that we're standing naked beneath flowing water.

"So you wouldn't do the same?" I ask, curious now as I lean against the marbled shower wall beside us.

"As her? No. Absolutely not." She sounds completely disgusted.

"What if you were told that the only way you could be accepted in Gold Sector was to present precious metals, like gold, to the court?" I press. "And an Alpha, or hell, *me*, what if I offered to give you gold in exchange for your child? Would you agree if it meant being accepted here?"

She gapes at me. "I'd rather go back to the nomad lands and take my chances with the Alphas there," she spits at me. "So if you think I'm going to agree to such a ridiculous arrangement, then you can fuck right off."

With that, she stomps toward the glass door and yanks it open with a growl that's all female wolf.

Damn if that doesn't make my knot throb.

I grab my cock and give it a stroke, a groan leaving me as I watch her sweet, curvy ass march out of the bathroom.

Soaking wet. Snarling. Vibrating with fury.

Because the very concept of abandoning her pup infuriates her.

This Omega is perfection.

Fucking. Perfection.

And I might have to make her mine…

CHAPTER ELEVEN

TALIANA

I... DIDN'T THINK THIS THROUGH.

Now I'm soaking wet in the middle of the Alpha's room with no towel, no clothes, and nowhere to go. But if he thinks I'm going to trade my firstborn for gold...

I snarl, snatching at the necklace around my neck.

Then the Prince of Gold Sector's words from earlier replay through my thoughts.

"Gold is a coveted metal in Gold Sector. I suggest you not only wear that necklace to your next audience with the court but also bring any other gifts you're given. The more items you can present, the better you'll be received. Do you understand?"

"Oh, Gods," I breathe. "I'm the miller's daughter..."

"You're nothing like her," Oros says as he saunters into the room with a large white towel. "Come here, printesa mea. You're dripping all over my wood floors."

I narrow my gaze at him. "I don't want anything from you. No more gold. No... no *towels*. Nothing. You are *not* taking my firstborn."

"I have no desire to take your firstborn," he murmurs, his steps bringing him closer to me and causing me to backpedal. I yelp as my rump hits his bed. He keeps coming toward me, making me wince against the mattress.

Only to be engulfed in the softest, fluffiest towel I've ever felt in my life.

He wraps it around me like it's a blanket, his strong arms yanking me away from his bed as he mutters, "I'm all for having a wet Omega in my bed, but not quite like this."

I shiver in his arms, his strength doing things to me. Things I want to reject. Things I want to *run* from.

Because I won't be the miller's daughter. I won't give up my child. *I won't be my mother*, I think, shuddering violently.

"Shh," he hushes.

But I won't be *shushed*.

"You can't have my child," I tell him.

My wolf seethes inside, furious right along with me. She might not understand our words or what we were discussing in the shower, but she understands me. And she's *livid*.

I can feel her clawing at my instincts, demanding I let her free.

It suddenly feels like my only option.

"Taliana," Oros says, a hint of dominance in his tone.

But I'm done listening to him. I... I can't be the miller's daughter. I won't be my mother. *I won't give up my child.*

Not for anything.

Not for being accepted.

Not for being mated.

Not for being wanted. Desired. *Claimed.*

No. I... I can't. I *won't*.

"*Taliana.*" His Alpha growl wraps around me, grounding me in the present and halting my shift before it can ignite. I cry out in agony at having his dominance pressing down on me, my knees bending in response.

He catches me and holds me, his purr instantly roaring to life as he presses his lips to my ear.

But I can't hear what he's saying.

My heart is beating too fast, my breathing a panting mess, my insides… *twisting*.

There's a low keening sound—a mewl?—that makes thought impossible. I… I just… I can't… I'm…

I'm blind.

Everything is dark.

No light.

No, too bright.

I wince, my hand covering my eyes as the world shifts all around me.

Blackness overtakes me once more, followed by a burning deep inside. Somewhere, someone is growling. Snapping. Arguing.

I… I don't know what to do. How to see. Where to go. *Who I am*. All I feel is *fire*. Intensity. *Heat*.

Gods…

It hurts. Oh, it's scorching me from the inside out. I think I'm crying. Screaming, maybe. Everything is wet. Scalding. *Fiery*.

But beneath it all, I sense a vibration that hypnotizes my wolf. She's been pacing inside me, mewling, screaming for a way out, but that hypnotic reverberation lulls her under a calming spell. I trace that rumble, needing more. It's so soothing. So tranquil. So *right*.

I nuzzle into it, my cheeks soaked with tears.

I'm still naked.

But hot. *So, so hot*.

"I've got you, Taliana," a familiar voice says, each word underscored with that intense purr. "Just try to relax for me, printesa mea. Can you do that, sweet girl? Take deep breaths. That's it. Inhale. Exhale. Inhale. Exhale."

I must be following his commands because I can feel the pressure alleviating in my chest.

"Good girl," he praises. "Keep breathing with me, little diamond. Yes, like that, baby. Exactly like that."

Dizziness overwhelms me, his words doing something to me deep within.

Maybe it's his nearness. His tone. His *scent*. I don't know, but all I want to do is nuzzle into him.

Except... except I shouldn't trust him. *Why, though?* I wonder. *Why can't I trust him?*

My head spins as I try to recall the reason, my mind foggy from whatever just happened.

Why am I so tired?

"I'm sorry I stopped your shift," he whispers against my ear. "Flames, that might have been the hardest thing I've ever had to do. But Doctor Taylor told you not to shift for a reason. You can't go into heat. Not until you have a plan in place."

I blink. *He used his Alpha dominance to quell my wolf.*

I can feel it now, my animal cowering inside me, terrified of the Alpha currently wrapped around me.

Or perhaps just scared because of what happened.

I try to pull away from him, needing to clear my mind, to recall exactly what occurred.

"I don't want your firstborn, Taliana," he says, confusing me even more.

What?

"It's a fairy tale. You asked about my nickname—Rumpel—and it's just because of my affinity for gold."

I finally open my eyes enough to look at him. Apparently, I'm in his lap. On the bed.

And we're both naked.

"It's an old joke my brother came up with when we were young," he goes on, his golden gaze grabbing and holding my focus. "He usually calls me Rumpelstiltskin when he wants to goad me. Just like I call him Silverstiltskin in return."

I keep staring at him, lost as to what any of this means.

"His affinity is for white gold," he goes on. "Referring to him as *Silverstiltskin* pisses him off. But I'm not exactly a fan of being compared to a conniving imp either."

"I don't…" I cough, my throat drier than I realized.

Oros reaches over for a bottle of water and brings it to my lips. I have no idea how that appeared nearby or why he had it ready, but I'm thankful anyway.

"I gave you that necklace as a sign of affection," he tells me. "Not because I expect something in return. And certainly not your firstborn. I would never take a child away from an Omega. That's cruel."

Okay, some of the earlier conversation is coming back to me now.

The shower.

His story.

The links my mind made to me being the miller's daughter.

I set the now-empty bottle of water aside and touch the coin hanging from my neck. "The Gold Sector Prince said gold is coveted," I whisper, recalling how my mind made the jumps earlier. "He told me it'll impress the Royal Court…" I try to yank on the chain again. "I don't want to impress them. I…"

"Taliana," he says, his hand covering mine. "This necklace isn't about impressing them. It's about me marking you."

I blink at that. "What?"

He blows out a breath, reminding me that I'm practically curled up in his lap because his chest is right next to my arm. "There's something about your scent that makes my dragon crazy. I made the necklace as a sign of favor, *my* favor, because I… I want you to wear my mark."

Frowning, I run my thumb over the coin and note the engraving. I can't tell what it is, exactly, but it's indented with some sort of symbol. "Oh."

"Oh," he echoes, huffing a laugh. "You have no idea how profound this is."

"Do guardians typically want their Omegas to wear their marks?" I ask slowly, trying to guess at what he means.

"No, little diamond. No, they do not. In fact, only Alphas courting an Omega mate do such a thing."

"Oh," I say again. Or, well, my lips form the shape. But it comes out barely audible.

Because Oros just insinuated that he made me this necklace… as a sign of courtship.

He wants me.

An Alpha… wants me.

And he knows about my wolf.

Which makes this even more impactful. Because a Drakonian Alpha wants to court me.

"I…" My brow furrows, my mind catching up on something else he said. "Because of my scent?" He said my scent was driving his dragon crazy.

"Yes," he answers without hesitation. "You smell like a field of wildflowers, one my dragon very much wants to roll in."

I blink at him. "You smell like a bonfire to me."

His nose wrinkles. "Is that good or bad?"

"Good," I tell him. "Very good." My cheeks heat at the admission, then burn when he smiles.

"Your father told me you're genetically predisposed to attract a mate by your scent," he informs me, causing my eyes to widen. "Or, well, it sounds like you may have inherited that trait from your mother, anyway."

My jaw tightens. "I'm nothing like my mother." The words come out angry. And they also remind me of how we ended up in this bed together. "My mother would have traded me for gold. She would have given me up for much less. *I am not my mother.*"

He gazes at me for a long moment, saying nothing. Then he nods. "I believe you."

Three words.

So simple.

Yet they... they release tension through my entire body.

I'm not even sure why it matters or why I needed to hear him say that. But I'm thankful for it anyway. Because it's... freeing.

"Thank you," I whisper. "Thank you for believing me."

He cants his head, his golden eyes glittering. "So what are we going to do, little diamond? Explore this connection between us? Or ignore it?"

My brow furrows. "Why would we ignore it? I... I came here for a mate."

"Because you actually want one? Or because you feel like you have no other option?"

"Um, I don't really have an option..." I reply, trailing off. Because what else is there to say?

"You do," he counters. "You don't have to accept a mate to stay here, Taliana."

"I'm pretty sure the Prince of Gold Sector would disagree with you," I inform him.

He laughs and shakes his head. "I'm actually quite certain that he would agree with everything I say, Taliana."

I arch a brow. "Yeah? That seems pretty cocky of you."

"Cocky?" he repeats. "Is that so?"

"Very." Although, I don't really mind. His confidence is refreshing. It makes him easy to trust. Easy to talk to. Easy to just… be around.

He chuckles again. "Well, I'm certain you have options, Taliana. If you don't want a mate, don't take one. But if you're open to exploring this chemistry between us, then I am, too."

I study him, noting the seriousness in his gaze. "Is it normal for a guardian to court an Omega?"

"It's not unheard of, but I wouldn't call it normal, either."

"Have you ever…?" I trail off, my attention returning to my necklace as I lift the coin. "Have you ever marked one of your charges before?"

"You're the only Omega I've ever volunteered to be a guardian for," he says, reaching for the token to stroke it with his fingertip. "You're also the first Omega I've ever given such a gift to."

I look at him again. "Really?"

"You don't believe me?"

"No, I'm just surprised," I admit.

He smiles, but it lacks the amusement of earlier. It's a different kind of smile. One that almost seems shy. "Trust me, none of this was intentional. But we're here now. You're in my bed. Naked. Wearing my gold. And all I want to do… is cover you in my scent."

"Because we're compatible," I say, repeating the term he used earlier.

"Yes."

"And you're offering to explore what that means," I reiterate.

"I am."

"Have you ever… explored with another Omega?"

"If you're asking if I've knotted Omegas before, then

yes, I have. But never with the intention of mating one. Only with the purpose of satisfying an Omega through her heat."

"But with me…?" I prompt him, wanting to make sure I understand the difference.

"With you, I want to explore everything," he says, his gaze falling to my lips. "I want to taste you. Knot you. Nest with you. Adorn you with gold. Learn everything about you. Fly with you." His eyes meet mine once more. "No one has ever appealed to me in this way, Omega. I want to see what this is, what we might be together."

I shiver, his honesty refreshing and also terrifying.

Because he's offering more than I've ever dreamed possible.

A future.

A potential pairing.

A Drakonian Alpha mate.

I would be a fool to say no to exploring more with him.

So I respond with the only words that make sense. "Okay. I accept your courtship, Alpha Oros."

CHAPTER TWELVE

OROS

It's on the tip of my tongue to correct her, to tell her my true title. But instinct holds me back. An instinct born of age and caution.

In my near millennium of life, I've never met an Omega like Taliana. A female I'm salivating over because of her scent alone.

My dragon is pounding at my chest, demanding that I claim this female. He's convinced she's mine.

But I don't know her.

Not yet.

She could still be a trap, just like her mother was for her father. Assuming that story is even true.

Although, her displeasure was palpable when she mentioned her mother. And thus far, everything she's told me felt truthful.

However, I need to be sure. One hundred percent certain. No room for doubt. Absolutely, positively clear on her intentions.

And I am nowhere near there yet.

Still, I have to start somewhere. Because this female might be my everything. My mate. *My future queen.*

Which means I have to give this a chance. To truly court her, just like I said.

Flames, Onyx is going to lose his shit when he finds out.

But I can't think about him right now. Not with the delectable Omega sitting in my lap, staring up at me with beautifully starry eyes.

She looks so hopeful, her gaze locked on me with a reverence I probably don't deserve.

But I can't question it.

I just want to embrace her. Experience the present. Indulge in this alluring Omega. And fucking kiss her.

Taliana's lips part like she knows my intent, her tongue sneaking out to dampen the flesh in glistening welcome.

I accept it for the invitation it is and lean down to claim her mouth.

She startles, telling me this is probably her first kiss.

Mmm, time to teach, then…

I've never been one to enjoy professor-type roles, but for her, I will happily assume the position of trainer.

Which is why I start slow, my tongue tracing her plump bottom lip, just like her tongue did moments ago. She gasps, the sound one I'll absolutely dream about later. Probably as I fantasize about her sucking my cock.

Fuck, my knot throbs at the concept.

I've been hard since walking into my suite and smelling her sweet perfume all over my quarters.

It's like she's claimed my space as her own. Or just pulled me under a spell.

That would explain so much.

But I'm not one to run from fate.

If this female is my future, I'll embrace her. Own her.

Keep her. *Possess* her. At least with my mouth and my hands.

Because, flames, this woman is my kryptonite. All soft, warm curves, and a mouth that's moving to my every command.

She's an apt pupil, her tongue mimicking mine as I deepen our kiss. I cup her jaw, holding her to me as my opposite arm goes around her waist. Then I carefully maneuver us on the bed so she's spread out beneath me, her naked body hot against my own.

Taliana doesn't react, too lost to our kiss to realize I've caged her in. But the moment my cock touches her slick heat, she jumps, her eyes widening. "Don't worry," I say against her mouth. "I'm not going to knot you tonight."

"You're n-not?" she asks, and I can't tell if she's confused or disappointed. Perhaps it's a mix of both.

"No, printesa mea," I murmur. "We'll ease into that." I trace her bottom lip with my tongue again. "This is about me taking care of you. Showing you how Alphas worship Omegas."

That's how this started—me wanting to bathe her.

Now I'm going to pleasure her.

Introduce her to sensations she's never experienced before.

Make her beg for my knot. Demand that I satisfy her during her heat. Leave her without question as to how thoroughly and expertly I can fuck her.

And ensure she desires me as much as I desire her.

I kiss her again, this time without the intent to teach, and only with the need to *own*.

She grabs my shoulders in response, her nails digging into my muscles, and holds on while I master her with my tongue.

I'm laying claim to her in a way I've never done before,

my beast urging me to do more, to devour her, take her, *mark* her.

Not just with my gold but also with my teeth.

It's a terrifying need, a foreign one that threatens my steadfast control.

Flames, if I'm losing my mind just kissing her, what am I going to do when I'm inside her?

I don't give myself a chance to find out, instead pulling my cock away from her weeping heat and ripping my mouth away from hers.

She's panting beneath me, her sweet slick permeating the air with an open invitation to *fuck*. Damn, she's so wet I could probably force myself inside her without even needing to prepare her.

Just the thought, the *notion*, of fucking her raw has my dick throbbing.

It makes controlling my needs so much more important.

I'll hurt her in this state.

Just because she could take me raw doesn't mean she should.

She's a virgin. Untouched. Inexperienced. You cannot have her. Not like this.

I press my lips to her throat as I mentally repeat those words, my mind shifting to a new task, one meant to focus on her. On pleasing her. On worshipping her. *On making her scream.*

She shudders beneath me, her nipples beading against my chest. "Oros," she whispers.

"Yes, printesa mea?" I ask, my mouth traveling down to her collarbone on my way to her breasts. "Do you want me to stop, Taliana?" I utter the question against her fleshy mound, my lips a scant inch from her stiff peak.

She stares down at me with lust-drunk eyes, her cheeks

a beautiful shade of crimson. "I… I don't want you to stop…"

"Good," I say, my mouth against her nipple now. "Let me know if that changes." I don't bother trying the safeword again. *Rumpel* was clearly the wrong choice earlier. And I really don't want to distract her.

Her lips part like she's about to say more, but the sound bites off on a moan as I lick her rosy tip. "Ohhh" is all that escapes her instead.

Smiling, I repeat the action, only this time I follow it up by closing my mouth around her and sucking.

"*Gods,*" she says, her hips arching up into my lower torso, which I settle more firmly between her splayed thighs, just to provide some friction.

"Not a God," I inform her, my mouth brushing her tit as I move to her opposite nipple. "Just a Drakonian. And I'll be the one praying today."

I bite down on her fleshy breast, not hard enough to bruise or wound, just hard enough to leave a red mark. Then I lave the pain away before tracing her areola with my tongue.

She writhes beneath me, her hips trapped under my much larger form. But I can tell by the way she jolts that she's enjoying being pinned.

Another moan parts her beautiful lips as I scrape my teeth along her breast. "I want to pierce your nipples with gold," I tell her softly. "Claim them with my metallic bite."

She shivers in response.

"I want to decorate every part of you in my power," I go on, kissing a path down to her flat abdomen. "I'll pierce you here, too." I like her belly button. "Create another charm for you to wear."

I've never done this with any Omega before, never even considered it a desire. But saying these things aloud now makes me realize how true these feelings are—I want her marked from head to toe. Pierced for my benefit. Wearing *my* gold.

Fuck, I can already picture it. Every gold adornment. Every mark. Every piece of me embedded in her flesh.

I nip her hip bone, loving the way it pinkens beneath my touch. Then continue my journey to the sweetness glistening between her thighs.

Fuck, I love this woman's scent.

It's particularly strong here, her slick a beacon to my dragon and enslaving my every need.

"I'm going to taste you, Omega," I warn her, my mouth nearing her clit. "I'm going to fucking *devour* you."

Her eyes widen, her lips parting in shock.

Then the most beautiful scream leaves her as I seal my mouth around her swollen flesh and *suck*.

CHAPTER THIRTEEN
TALIANA

OH, GODS... OH, GODS... OH...

I'm on fire in the best way.

Burning beneath Oros's skilled mouth. Lost to his touch. His words. His *everything*.

He's between my legs. Oh, my Gods, he's between my legs...

And not with his knot. But his *tongue*.

I... I never...

A moan that sounds part wolf vibrates through me, the growl underscoring it all feral need. I've never explored myself much, my suppressants having stunted me in a lot of ways. But oh, I like this exploration now.

Foreign flames flood my veins, my core alive with a cyclone of intense sensations. It curls within me, making me dizzy with *want*.

Oros said he wasn't going to knot me. I don't understand why, and at first, I was somewhat relieved. But now... now I want... something. Anything. Pressure. *Inside me.*

I say his name as his palms slide up my thighs, his mouth still focused on my sensitive flesh. He's found some sort of pleasurable spot, one that throbs and pulses against his tongue.

My clit, I think, fairly certain that's the term. But I've never had cause to discuss it.

Until now. Until him. Until *this*.

Only, it's not enough. "I need more," I tell him, the words falling unbidden from my lips. I don't know what they mean. Or what I'm actually craving. But I'm hoping he understands.

"You need me inside you," he says, his gold irises finding mine as his fingers prod at my damp center. "Like this."

My lips part on a scream as he enters me, the pain transforming into instant pleasure as he moves his finger—no... *fingers*—in a hypnotic pattern deep within my tight channel.

My toes curl as he strokes a particular spot, stars shooting off behind my eyes and blinding my vision.

"Mmm, that's it, Taliana," he murmurs. "Glisten for me, little diamond."

Every part of me clenches, his erotic words doing something to me.

His comments about piercing me ignited a fire inside my soul, one his praise now is stoking even hotter. I have no idea who I am. But my wolf is roaring through me, guiding me to the precipice of an unknown oblivion.

"Flames, printesa mea, the way you're squeezing my fingers is making me want to fuck you," he breathes. "You're going to feel so fucking good around my cock, take my knot so damn well."

Each word is spoken against my clit, the vibrations stirring invisible waves of electricity that hum along my skin.

"I feel..." I can't finish my sentence. I don't know how

to describe what I'm experiencing. *Life? Pleasure? A renewed existence?*

"Are you hot all over?" he asks me, his voice a rumble of sound that he emphasizes with his purr.

"Yes," I breathe.

"Like you're about to explode?"

I nod frantically, my teeth sinking into my bottom lip as I mumble out a choked sound of agreement.

"Ride that wave, little diamond," he tells me, his tongue slipping out to tease my swollen flesh. His fingers pump deep, twisting and turning inside me, making me feel full yet empty at the same time. "Ride it until you crash."

I don't know what he means, but I try to do what he says, my body balancing on the precipice of something catastrophic.

His mouth clamps down on me again, sending me into the stars and forcing me over the edge into madness.

I lose my sight.

My sense of sound.

My… my everything.

It's all so intense. So beautiful. So *amazing*.

Ripples of pleasure warm me from head to toe, my body pulsing in time with his tongue. His lips. His touch. His *being*.

We're connected. One. Writhing in a pool of rapture, existing on a plane I can't even begin to define.

And suddenly, I'm… I'm me again. Blinking up at the white ceiling. Clutching the plush bedding beneath me. Panting like I just sprinted for miles through a dark forest.

A jolt echoes up from between my thighs as Oros kisses me there, then his big, powerful body crawls up over me, his mouth wet with my arousal.

He doesn't say anything, just kisses me. Forces me to

taste myself on his tongue. Indulges me with my own pleasure. And settles once more between my thighs, his hardness aligning perfectly with my weeping heat. Only, he doesn't enter me. He simply… relaxes.

With his head against my clit.

And his knot pulsing much farther down.

I can feel his need, taste his desire, sense his feral nature.

Yet he kisses me with a reverence I feel warming every inch of my soul.

"That, my darling Omega, is how Alphas treat our females here," he tells me softly. "Now I'm going to make you come again with my cock because I want you to saturate my skin with your sweet scent."

My lips part, questions firing in my mind, but he kisses me before I can formulate the words out loud.

Suddenly his tongue is possessing mine, teaching me a new dance, one where he leads and I follow. Because why wouldn't I follow? He's igniting my soul in a way I never knew was possible.

When his hips press down, my legs shift to wrap around him. It's the most natural response in the world, one I fully embrace as I start rubbing myself against him, coating his hardness with my arousal and moaning each time he applies pressure to my clit.

Gods, this is…. so unlike me. I feel animalistic. Feral. Lost to the savagery within.

But I can't stop it.

I just want more.

I want him.

I need to know this, to experience that heat again, to *fly*.

Gods, that's it, I realize. *Falling off that cliff must be similar to soaring through the clouds.*

Yes, I need that to happen again.

Oh, Gods, yes…

I clutch his shoulders, my body going up in flames beneath him as I chase the pleasure zipping through my being. "*Oros.*" His name comes out on a hiss of sound, one that ends in a groan as I tumble into that blissful oblivion once more.

Only this time, I can feel him rubbing up against me, his heat a blanket that leaves me feeling protected and safe as I fall even deeper into the cloud of eroticism.

So hot.

So explosive.

So wonderful.

By the time I settle, I realize we're kissing. Except the movement is slower now, his lips whispering against mine, his touch gentle along my sides. He's also purring, his contentment lulling me into a state of sweet relaxation.

I yawn, suddenly exhausted.

My eyes flutter closed. *Just a few minutes*, I tell myself. *I'll rest… for just a few minutes.*

His nose traces my cheek, his lips ghosting across my skin. "You can rest for as long as you need, printesa mea," he says softly.

Hmm, I must have said those words out loud.

Oh well.

I nuzzle into him, belatedly realizing that I'm somehow snuggled into his side now. It doesn't matter. He's purring. My nose is near his chest.

For the first time in forever, I feel safe.

Warm.

And perfectly… content.

CHAPTER FOURTEEN
OROS

THERE'S AN OMEGA IN MY BED.

It's a realization that wakes me with a start, my knot instantly throbbing with awareness.

Because the little female is curled up against my side, sleeping soundly.

I didn't mean to fall asleep beside her. But it doesn't appear to be feasible to have any intentions around Taliana. Because it's clear that nothing in this fated arrangement is predictable.

Including my instincts.

I've never brought an Omega into my quarters, let alone into my bed.

I never wanted to encourage nesting.

Yet now I'm disappointed to find the bed mostly untouched.

Onyx said Taliana was considering making a nest in my bed. Taliana also confirmed that desire.

However, I see no evidence of that interest. And I find that strangely disconcerting.

I pleased her. I know I did. So why isn't she nesting?

Maybe she just needs rest, I decide, noting her relaxed form. *So beautiful. Alluring. Perfect. And mine.*

My chest aches at that last thought.

The urge to mark her remains, my gold around her neck not enough.

I need to go for a flight. Stretch my wings. Think.

Otherwise, I'm going to do something rash.

A little late for that, I decide, glancing down at the pretty Omega.

So leaving is a good idea before I make another *rash* decision, then.

Taking a deep breath, I prepare to maneuver away from the addictive female in my bed. She shifts a little as I move, her head stealing my pillow to burrow into the soft silk.

I still as she inhales deeply, like she's as addicted to my scent as I am to hers.

Then she settles on a sigh, clearly content once more.

Hmm, I hum to myself, admiring the view of her naked body in my bed. *I want to keep her in this state.*

Not just naked, but pleased.

Stalking over to my en-suite kitchen, I consider the contents of the fridge and pick out some items for her.

Fresh fruit.

Cheese.

Water.

I arrange it all—slicing the berries into a bowl and cutting up some cheese on a plate that I line with crackers —and set everything on a tray with a glass for her drink.

Almost perfect, I think, searching for a pen and paper. Yesterday, she expressed concern over her intruding on my space. I make it clear in a few words that my suite is her suite and she's welcome to do whatever she wants here.

Satisfied with my gift, I walk over to place it on the nightstand, then frown.

Something is still missing.

I pull the blankets up to tuck her in, my gaze catching on her necklace along the way. My lips curl, my inner beast pleased by the placement of our mark.

Seeing it also provokes an idea, one I'm already working on before the thought completes in my mind.

Gold weaves between my fingers, the magic familiar and warm as a cuff appears in my hand, one that suits Taliana's much smaller wrist.

A symbol glitters up at me, the one I know well—a lotus flower with flame-like petals. My family emblem.

I set the bracelet down on the tray, then grab the note I wrote and add a few more words to it about my gift.

Right, now *it's perfect.*

Pleased, I step away from the bed, my gaze on my female.

She doesn't stir or react, too lost to her dreams to notice I'm slowly creeping backward out of the room. I don't take my eyes off of her until I reach the balcony closest to my bed. Then I search the sky and note the dawning sun. I obviously fell asleep for hours, which explains my dragon's burning need for a flight.

Well, the Omega in our bed is part of that burning need, too.

But I usually go on night patrols, enjoying the starry evening sky around the midnight hour. And I missed that opportunity while sleeping with Taliana in my bed.

So a morning scout it is.

I run forward and jump into the sky as fire flows through my veins, my dragon instantly taking the reins over our form.

The shift isn't immediate, but it's not slow either.

Within seconds, we're soaring through the sky, our wings sprawling to control our free fall.

My dragon huffs as our dive turns into a spin that pivots us upward.

And then we take off toward the horizon.

My mind settles with each passing moment, Taliana's scent lost to the wind ripping around me. I feel free. Properly able to think. To *process* everything that's happened.

Yet deep down, I feel unsettled in a way I've never experienced before.

I love to fly, to explore alone with my dragon and simply exist without having to worry about anyone or anything else.

However, the freedom I often crave isn't nearly as inviting or pleasing as it has been in the past.

Because she's not here.

Her missing scent... is no longer satisfying. It's troubling instead.

I miss her, I realize, startled by the epiphany. *How can I miss someone I just met?*

Drakonians are covetous by nature, and we're strongly possessive of our mates. But she isn't mine. Not yet.

I'm not even sure I want to claim her.

Which is a lie, I suppose. I've already marked her in a way I've never marked anyone.

Fuck. My dragon growls as though agreeing with the curse. Then he growls for an entirely different reason as a pair of silver wings flash in the rising sun. *Onyx.*

It's not uncommon for my brother to join me on a flight, but not quite like this. And especially not this early in the morning.

Sighing, I tell my dragon to follow his.

And naturally, my brother leads us to the landing outside my office.

I inhale deeply as I shift back into my human form, my short flight nowhere near satiating my animal's needs. Yet he appears to be pacified by something else entirely now— our Omega's scent.

Because we're right below my suite here.

There's even a set of stairs outside that leads up to the outdoor platform framing my quarters.

"Sorry," my brother says as he grabs some pants from the stash in my closet. He tosses a pair to me before bending to pull the other up his long legs, our sizes nearly identical. "I wouldn't interrupt your flight without cause."

I hum, aware that he obviously has something important to share. But I can't help ribbing him a bit. "The last flight you interrupted was to tell me an Alpha was requesting an audience with the court to discuss his Omega daughter. And look how that turned out."

"You smell like her, so I'm going to say it didn't turn out all that badly," my brother returns.

I grunt. Although, he's not wrong. I do smell like her. Fuck, I can still taste her on my tongue. Just thinking about it has me very carefully zipping up my pants, my knot throbbing to life in an instant. "What's happened now?" I ask, needing his news to distract me from thinking about the Omega lying in my bed.

He takes a deep breath, telling me without words that this is going to be bad. "Our scouts in Azores Sector reached out. Obsidian Sector just claimed Lanzarote as their own."

I was halfway to my office bar when my brother dropped that last sentence, causing me to stop mid-step and spin toward him. "*What*? How the fuck did they get through Gibraltar?" Because I know Riordan didn't let

Prince Basalt and his merry band of Alpha fuckwits through.

"It's unclear," my brother hedges, clearing his throat. "But I think they went through Djinn Sector."

My stomach clenches at the mention of the infamous smokelike creatures known for having taken over the deserts of the North Africa region. *Djinn Sector* was commonly considered to be the center of that world, Alpha Aisha the renowned Queen of the Djinn.

"If Aisha and Basalt have aligned," I begin, swallowing as an array of possibilities slam into my thoughts, none of them good. I sum them all up with a succinct "*Fuck*."

"Yes." My brother walks around me to the bar and pours both of us a double shot of lavaball. I down the drink in one go, slamming the glass on the gold-coated counter. Onyx instantly refills it, then drinks his own.

It's not even eight in the morning, and we're both drinking the hard shit. "We need to talk to Riordan."

"I've already reached out. Just waiting for him to call back."

I nod and stalk over to my desk, my screens appearing in the air as I sit down. There are four of them, all translucent until I reach for one. They're sensitive to touch, their magic tangible as I call up my messages.

Nothing from Riordan.

But I know he's seen and read my latest missive. The Alpha practically lives on his devices, making it impossible for him to have gone this long without seeing my note.

Hmm. "Do you think it's a coincidence that Riordan sent us his spy and Basalt has somehow slipped through the seas to reach Lanzarote, all at the same time?" I ask my brother.

"I really don't think Riordan let him through

Gibraltar," my brother says. "He hates Basalt even more than we do."

"Yet Rio apparently let Alpha Keegan remain there for fires know how long," I point out.

When Keegan told me about the arrangement yesterday, I originally assumed Riordan allowed him to stay there because he wanted Keegan to spy on Obsidian Sector.

What if it was all prearranged? I wonder now. *What if Rio's hatred for Basalt was a front for something else entirely?*

Impossible, I think in the next beat. *I would have sensed—*

"You're assuming Alpha Keegan is telling you the truth," my brother says, interrupting my mental debate regarding Rio's motives.

"I do have a knack for sniffing out lies," I remind him coolly.

"But is your ability working properly right now?" he counters, making my eyes narrow.

"What are you implying?" I ask, wanting him to lay all his cards on the table. "If you're going to insult me, at least be thorough."

He grunts at that and collapses into his favorite chair across from me. "You let an unknown Omega into your quarters, brother. Yet you've never let any other Omega up there, including the ones you've knotted through several heats."

My jaw ticks. He's not wrong. But I don't like what he's suggesting. "My ability is working just fine." Although, my senses are arguably occupied by Taliana's perfume.

However, lies always smell like burnt rubber.

That stench would absolutely override her alluring scent.

"Is it?" he presses, referring back to my claim regarding

my talent for distinguishing truth from fiction. "Tell me what you smell right now."

"I'm not trying to scent lies at the moment."

"Not the point."

I sigh and swipe my hand through the air, clearing my desk of the translucent screens so I can catch and hold my brother's stare. "Can I smell her right now? Yes. But she's literally above my head."

"Yet all I smell is her residual claim on your skin and nothing more," he tells me, his hand moving in a way that suggests he just made his point. "She's captivated your senses, Oros. At least acknowledge that. Then we can discuss what cause Keegan has to lie. Her, too."

I swallow, not liking the trajectory of this conversation. "You're suggesting she's here as a distraction from whatever Basalt is up to. And you're insinuating that Rio might be in on it. Except you also said you don't think he let them through Gibraltar."

"Because I don't think Rio is in on anything," he says. "But I don't think Keegan and his daughter are here by error. The timing is too suspicious, as is your sudden infatuation with her."

I frown at him. "Keegan said he was old friends with Riordan."

"And you believe him," my brother replies. "I don't."

My brow furrows even more. "Why?"

"Because it's too convenient. And, returning to your question regarding coincidences, no, I don't find it to be a coincidence at all. I think Keegan and his daughter are here as a distraction, just like you insinuated. And now we're finding out why the distraction was needed."

"To keep us from reacting to Basalt's movements," I say.

Onyx nods, his silver hair flickering in the early

morning rays of the sun streaming in from the balcony. "He probably thought you would be too deep into knotting the little Omega to see or hear reason." My brother leans forward. "He severely underestimated your control."

"Or you're wrong and this really is a coincidence."

He lifts a shoulder. "I guess we'll find out when Riordan returns my call."

I consider him and my hidden screens once more. "He never replied to my message." Which I already decided was strange, but now... now I'm even more concerned. "I asked about his pet spy."

"So you might have offended him," my brother translates.

"Maybe." I settle back into my chair again. "But it wouldn't be the first time. And he loves to prove me wrong. Why not use this opportunity to do so?"

"Perhaps he's concerned that you've fallen into a trap?" Onyx suggests, arching a brow. "Have you?"

I snort. "I'm sitting here talking to you. What do you think?"

"I think you smell like a claimed Alpha," he replies without missing a beat. "I know you weren't foolish enough to give in to her pussy that easily, but I have concerns."

My dragon instantly growls, not liking my brother's crass words. "Careful," I warn him.

"That," he says, gesturing to me. "*That* is why I have concerns. You don't know her, Oros. Yet you've half lost your mind over her already."

"You don't know if she's a trap or not," I remind him flatly. "You're guessing."

"And you're defending something that should be a huge fucking red flag," he retorts. "I'm your Second for a reason, Oros. Remember that."

"Are you threatening me?" I ask, startled by the conviction in his tone.

"No. I'm reminding you of who I am and why you put me in this position. If that female drugs your senses, I will handle the problem. That's my job."

"So you're threatening her," I realize aloud, standing. "Don't you fucking touch—"

A knock at my office door pauses me mid-shout, causing both me and my brother to glance at the threshold.

One sniff tells me who it is, and I'm already sighing as she enters without waiting for me to answer her knock.

Bella Chambers.

The Omega I last knotted.

I glare at my brother, certain he's the reason she's here.

He thinks I've lost my mind over Taliana Embers, and maybe I have. But calling this Omega up here is *not* the solution.

I'm going to fucking kill you, I tell him with a look.

His trademark amusement is missing. Instead, he has the grace to look alarmed. Good. He should be alarmed.

Because I don't have patience for tests or games.

I'm the Gold Sector Prince.

No Omega will ever change that.

CHAPTER FIFTEEN

TALIANA

A Few Minutes Earlier

GOOSE BUMPS PEBBLE ACROSS MY ARMS AND LEGS, MY MIND instantly alert.

Something doesn't feel right.

I went from being warm to suddenly cold.

Alone.

My eyes open, the black sheets around me unfamiliar. Yet the scent is one that makes my wolf rumble with approval.

Mmm. Alpha. My Alpha.

I bury my nose in the nearest pillow, memories of Oros filling the void behind my eyes. Him between my legs. Licking me. Touching me. Making me *fly*.

I shiver, then moan as sensations awaken deep inside me. I want more of that, more of *him*.

But he's not here. *He's…* I roll to my back, searching the space for him. *He's gone.*

Frowning, I push myself up from the heavenly bed and

study the tray on the nightstand. A note is folded between a plate and something gold.

I reach for the letter first, wanting to see if it says where Oros went.

Good morning, printesa mea,
I've slipped out to stretch my wings.
Nest. Eat. Do whatever makes you comfortable. I'll be back soon.
Yours,
Oros
PS: I made you something special. Please wear it for me.

I read the missive twice, my lips curling each time I see the word *nest*. Because yes. Yes, please. I very much want to do that.

Except... there's a scent that isn't quite right. Something a bit too sweet. I lean down to sniff the blankets, frowning when I can't determine the irritating note in the air. *Strange.* I search every part of his bed, all of it bathed in bonfire and ash and... and *me*.

I smile again, pleased.

Until that too-sweet perfume tickles my nose again.

My wolf huffs inside, not liking it one bit. *Another Omega?* I wonder, slipping from the sheets, my nose leading my steps.

It grows stronger when I reach the balcony outside his bedroom, causing my eyes to narrow.

Competition lurks nearby, I recognize, annoyed by the intrusion. *Where are you? Who are you?*

I prowl forward, my animal driving my instincts as we wander outside into the sun. The warmth on my skin gives me momentary pause. *I'm naked.*

But that scent...

I need to find the source of it. Get rid of it. *Remove her.*

A growl lingers in my chest as I find a set of stairs that leads down to another platform. I can *hear* her now, her soft voice reaching my ears, thanks to my wolf's enhanced senses.

"My next heat is in five weeks," she's saying, making me nearly miss a step. "I wanted to ask if you're willing to help me through it again, Alpha."

"Bella," a familiar voice murmurs in reply, the endearment one I've heard many times in my life. It's Italian. And it's a term Alphas in Obsidian Sector often used when inviting an Omega in to play.

My feet falter, my heart suddenly in my throat.

"I know, I know. It's early for the request, but I haven't been able to stop thinking about your knot," the Omega practically purrs, and I can picture her touching my Alpha as she talks about his *knot*.

Which has me almost jumping down the stairs to see her. To confront her. *To challenge her.*

A yelp leaves me as my bare skin snags on the concrete texture of the stairs, my human side warring with my wolf's needs.

Because this is insane.

He's not mine. He might be courting me, but Alphas take multiple Omega mates. I know that. I've *seen* it. That's the natural course of everything.

So who am I to run down here and challenge the Omega propositioning Oros?

If anything, I'm the intruder here, something her echoing words in my mind confirm.

Willing to help me through it again, Alpha.

He's... he's knotted her before. During a different heat. And now she—

A gasp comes from my right, making me wince.

Because yeah, I'm... on the bottom stair. My wolf won the battle inside me, forcing me toward Oros despite my human side shouting reason.

She's a possessive beast.

And she's… growling.

Which is probably what made the other Omega gasp.

I close my eyes and fight the violence clawing at my insides. Shifting right now would be very bad. Not only would it be inappropriate, but it would also probably end in Oros removing his protection.

I have no right to interfere with his personal affairs.

Except, his note said—

Energy swirls around me, causing my lashes to flutter in surprise.

My gaze instantly meets a pair of striking golden orbs. *My Alpha.*

No. Not *my* Alpha. He's… he's…

"Cloak," he bites out.

My brow furrows. *Cloak?*

More energy warms the air as an Alpha appears beside us. One glance has my eyes widening in shock. *Voice.*

My gaze instantly drops to the ground.

Oh, Gods. Not only did I just make a fool of myself in front of Oros, but the Gold Sector Prince witnessed it, too.

And I can't even begin to explain myself.

Sorry, my wolf is possessive isn't an excuse either Alpha will find acceptable.

Wolves are inferior to dragons. And I'm an Omega. Both are slights against me, ones that give me no right to any sort of possessive claim over Oros.

No right to *growl* at another female.

An apology lingers on my lips, yet I can't seem to voice it. Because I don't know how to explain my behavior without mentioning my animal.

And surely the prince won't approve of my wolf. Oros might not mind, but a royal Drakonian definitely will.

I'm still trying to speak as a soft fabric surrounds my

shoulders, the texture reminding me of my visit with Doctor Taylor yesterday.

Only, this isn't the same cloak. This is a new one. Something I know because the other one was left in the suite.

Unless he brought it down here while I slept?

No. It's missing my scent. So it must be another one of Oros's cloaks.

My wolf preens inside at the concept of being given more of his clothes.

But I can't seem to bring myself to meet his gaze.

Because I know he's furious with me. How could he not be?

His hands run over my trembling form, swathing me completely in his cloak. Magic warms my skin as he creates little gold adornments that function as clips to hold the fabric together down my torso.

I frown at the display of power, surprised he's going to such lengths to cover me.

His fingers clasp my jaw when he's done, his grip surprisingly gentle as he guides my eyes up to his. I flinch inside, dreading what I'll find…

Except…

He studies me, his eyebrows angled down. Not in a disapproving way, but in a way that indicates concern. "Are you all right?"

I blink at him. "I…" I have no idea how to reply to that. He's asking if I'm all right? After the spectacle I just made of myself?

"Bella," he says, making me wince. I much prefer his *printesa mea* nickname for me. "You should go."

My gaze falls despite his hold on my chin. "Oh, right. Okay," I whisper, his command one I expected. His perceived concern was obviously a fluke, something I foolishly misinterpreted.

Gods, why is this—

"I wasn't talking to you, little diamond," he murmurs, forcing my gaze back up to his. "I was talking to Omega Bella." He glances at the gorgeous blonde female standing about ten feet away, her eyes bright with surprised confusion.

Wow, I think, marveling at her beauty. *She's like a Goddess.*

And very clearly a purebred dragon.

I can see the beast staring at me through her vivid blue irises.

"Bella," he says again, this time with a hint of demand.

She takes a flinching step backward. "I'm sorry, My—"

"I'll escort you out, Bella," Voice interrupts, stepping between us and cutting off my view of the Omega. He moves forward with fluid movements, his torso as rippled with muscle as Oros's, the two of them only wearing pants.

But I barely have a second to notice his athletic physique before Oros pulls me into a kiss, his mouth possessive and hot against mine.

It's so unexpected that I freeze.

However, the second his tongue touches mine, I melt. He wraps his arms around me, his scent bathing me in a fiery claim I feel to my very soul. By the time he releases me, I'm panting and dizzy and nearly consumed by passion.

Except that female's perfume still lingers in the air, making my wolf growl. A sound I can't quite swallow.

Once again, I find myself incapable of apologizing even though I know I should. But Oros simply looks amused.

"Your animal is possessive," he muses, holding me

close. "Mmm, I think I like that, printesa mea." He leans down to nip at my bottom lip. "My dragon feels similarly."

"I'm trying to control her," I grumble, hating that I can't. And also hating that I... I don't really want to.

Something is fundamentally wrong with me.

I struggled to submit in Obsidian Sector, too. But I learned my place. Only to have every intrinsic rule and instinct broken while in the nomad lands.

"Please don't," Oros replies, his hand leaving my chin to cup my jaw. "I find your wolf pretty fucking sexy." He places another kiss on my lips. "And I'm sorry about Bella. I didn't know she was coming up for a visit, nor did I invite her into my office."

"You don't have to explain yourself to me," I tell him. "I... I'm familiar with Alphas and their, um, harem." I twist my mouth to the side, hating the word *harem*. "I'm aware that Alphas court multiple Omegas." There. That... that summarizes what I meant to say.

Although, *court* is a relatively new term, one I adopted because he used it yesterday. But it gets the point across.

Except he jerks back like I've slapped him.

"*What?*" he demands, causing me to also take a step back.

Only, he charges toward me as I do, his hand suddenly around my nape as his opposite arm encircles my waist.

"*No.* We will *not* be courting others. I do not share, Omega."

I gape at him. "I... I wouldn't..." I'm so confused. "Alphas court multiple Omegas. Not the other way around. I know that. I know better than to see more than one Alpha."

There were a few Omegas permitted that privilege in Obsidian Sector—my mother being one of them—but I wasn't a dragon. I would never have been forced to take multiple Alpha mates.

And thank the Gods for that.

Oros takes a deep breath, then lets it out so slowly that I wonder if he's counting down in his head. Because I've clearly upset him. *Again.*

Or maybe not again?

I… I'm still unclear about what just happened here on this balcony.

I interrupted him with another Omega, and he—

"Gold Sector Alphas do not court multiple Omegas." He utters the words with such measured calm that I can't help but shiver.

Because he's furious.

I can feel his fury now, taste it in the air, see it dancing in his gaze.

Yet his palm on my nape isn't tense, and his arm around my waist is relaxed.

Somehow, he's holding all that anger back. And I have no idea why.

"I want to take you on a tour today," he goes on. "It's very clear to me that you need to see how things are done here. Because this is *not* Obsidian Sector. And I am not an Obsidian Sector Alpha. I'm a real fucking Drakonian Alpha. And I will only ever court one Omega. *You.*"

CHAPTER SIXTEEN
OROS

Naturally, my brother chooses that exact moment to appear behind Taliana.

His nostrils flare at my declaration, the words powerful and laden with meaning.

Fortunately, he doesn't remind me that I only just met this Omega.

Unfortunately, said Omega is gaping at me with a mixture of confusion and awe.

When she mentioned courting others, my dragon roared with fury and nearly had me pinning her beneath me.

We will not share, my beast wanted me to say. *You. Are. Ours.*

But then it became clear that she expected me to entertain multiple Omega mates. And that... *that* insulted my ego.

I'm a fucking Drakonian Alpha.

And not just any Drakonian Alpha, but a Godsdamn *prince*.

I want one mate. One Omega. Not a flaming harem.

So yeah, I said some things. Things my brother overheard. Things he's no doubt judging me for now.

But I won't take them back.

Courting isn't the same as claiming.

I can *court* for as long as I desire. Days. Months. Years. Whatever it takes to establish trust between me and Taliana.

My dragon might prefer the courtship to last hours. But I'm in charge here, not him.

"Bella Chambers is my past," I add aloud, feeling like I need to explain what Taliana just witnessed. "An Omega I saw through a few heats. I never courted her, and I never intend to court her. That's not how things are done here." Something she'll understand better after our tour. "Let's—"

My suggestion is cut off by a buzzing on my wrist, my watch alerting me of an incoming call.

I curse when I see the name.

Taking Taliana on a tour is important, but meeting with Riordan is imperative. I can't delegate this conversation to my brother.

I also can't seem to bring myself to release Taliana either, though.

So instead, I tug her into me for a quick kiss and say, "I need to take this call."

She nods and swallows, her feet already pulling her away from me.

But I catch her hand and guide her right back to me. "We'll take it in my office."

My brother gives me a look of disapproval but smartly keeps his mouth shut. I'll deal with him after we talk to Rio.

Swiping my thumb over my watch, I accept the incoming message. The Prince of Jasper Sector appears in front of me on a translucent screen that moves as I walk. His dark hair is braided in a series of rows along his scalp, allowing me to see the wolf tattoo decorating the side of his head. There are several Viking runes, too.

And something new.

"Nice web," I tell him, referring to the small spiderweb etched into the corner of his forehead.

He doesn't immediately reply, his focus on the Omega walking beside me. "Helena?" he asks, sounding shocked.

Taliana's gaze instantly flies upward, her eyes widening in alarm.

"Holy shit," Rio breathes, causing my footsteps to falter.

My brother and I frown at each other, then down at the Omega, who is gaping at the screen. "Helena?" I repeat, my heart suddenly kick-starting in my throat.

But before I can worry about any lies Taliana may have given me regarding her identity, I recall my conversation with her father.

"Your mother," I acknowledge aloud in the next moment.

"You look just like her," Rio adds unhelpfully. "But your eyes are all Keegan. Same shape. Though, the starburst pattern is missing some of the white."

"Stop studying my Omega," I demand.

Rio's eyebrow lifts as he finally shifts his gaze to me. "*Your* Omega?"

My jaw ticks, my hand tightening around Taliana's as I start walking again. "How do you know my father?" she asks, her bold question almost making me stumble.

It seems the submissive Omega from moments ago has disappeared, and in her place is a woman with suspicion etched into her beautiful features.

As she holds Rio's gaze with the intensity and confidence of a fellow Alpha.

A queen, I think, pleased. *Very* pleased.

Although, it's interesting that she didn't ask how he knew her mother. Only her father.

"Do you know who I am?" Rio asks her, his tone more curious than arrogant.

"No. Should I?"

He smiles. "You should, but that's not your fault so much as your father's. I'll be sure to comment on it the next time we speak."

"So you admit he's one of your spies?" I interject, somewhat relieved to hear he knows Keegan—because that proves the Alpha told me some truths yesterday. But I'm also equal parts wary, given what it all means.

"I would never send such an obvious plant, Golden Boy," Rio drawls, using a nickname I despise even more than Rumpel and Rumpelstiltskin. "You know me better than that."

I snort. "Didn't you once tell me the most obvious enemies are the ones standing right in front of you?"

He grins at the mention of a conversation we had over a century ago when the Infection began to spread through the human masses.

It was a memorable talk, one that allied us for over a hundred years.

I hope that alliance isn't about to crash and burn today.

But it will. Especially if I find out he's been working with Basalt all along.

Onyx silently takes his favorite chair while I settle in the one beside him and drag Taliana into my lap. The gold clasps thankfully keep her cloak closed, hiding her beautiful body from Riordan's view. But that doesn't stop him from casting another appreciative glance her way.

Something I ensure he knows I noticed by shooting him a look.

Which earns me another grin.

"I had no idea you could smile so much," I tell him.

"And I had no idea our conversations were memorable enough for you to recite my words verbatim," he retorts. "But I'm glad to hear they had a lasting impact." His smile is gone as he leans forward to add, "Because I think we have some important items to discuss, and trust is going to be imperative."

I hum, agreeing with him.

"But before we get to that," he goes on, his focus returning to my Omega. "My name is Riordan."

She stiffens. "The Jasper Sector Prince."

"One and the same," he murmurs. "But you can call me Uncle Rio if you prefer."

"Keegan's your brother?" I ask, sharing a look with my own brother. We at least have the same stature and similar facial structures.

But Keegan and Rio look nothing alike.

Keegan also failed to mention the familial link.

"If she's your niece, why did you send her here?" Onyx adds, suspicion deepening his tone. Probably because this is all beginning to feel more and more like a trap.

Yet all Rio does is sigh. "He's not my blood brother. But he is my best friend."

"Then my question still stands," Onyx grinds out. "Why send them here? Why not accept them into Jasper Sector?"

"You know why," Rio bites back to him, his tone considerably sharper as he speaks each word through his teeth. "Jasper Sector is full of purists."

"Seems convenient as far as excuses go," my brother says, clearly unimpressed. "But I guess that's standard where you're concerned."

Riordan's gaze narrows. "I won't tolerate your brand of verbal sparring this early in the morning, Silver Kiss."

"Fuck you, Red Rock."

I rub the bridge of my nose, a headache forming behind my eyes. This is how these chats always go when Rio and Onyx are on a call. It starts with ridiculous nicknames and ends with true insults.

They're far too similar and therefore push each other's buttons without even trying.

As they're both Alphas—and powerful ones at that— neither ever backs down.

Requiring me to be the voice of reason.

Except I'm not the one who speaks next.

Instead, it's a small feminine voice filled with curiosity that says, "My father has told me a lot about you, Uncle Rio. And he explained why we couldn't go to his home sector. I understand why I won't be accepted there. My wolf is inferior to the dragons."

"Your wolf is not inferior," I interject. "I can't believe your father told you that."

I may have to fucking kill him for it, too.

All shifters are powerful in their own right.

Drakonians may possess some superior qualities, but there are things wolves can do that dragons cannot.

Like sprint through the woods.

"My father doesn't feel that way, but he's warned me that others do. And Obsidian Sector…" She trails off, then shakes her head. "My point is, I know why my father and I didn't go to Jasper Sector. It was too far for us to travel, and my father knew I wouldn't be accepted as a worthy Omega mate."

She shrugs in a way that says "What can you do?" And it infuriates me.

"You're worthy," I tell her. "And fuck anyone who says otherwise."

Rio clears his throat, the bastard not so subtly reminding me of his virtual presence.

Like I could fucking forget.

"Oros is right, *cariño*. You're extremely worthy. Which is why I suggested Gold Sector to your father. I knew the Alphas there would treat you with the respect you deserve. Their Omega relocation resources are the most robust in the region, and they're not afraid to embrace Omegas from alternative backgrounds."

I stare at the male whom I once considered to be my rival. "I'm willing to forgive you for calling her *sweetheart* because of everything you just said about my sector. But don't push your luck again."

The asshole's lips twitch. "I'm not sure if I should be amused by your possession or concerned."

"The latter," my brother mutters. "Definitely the latter. But I assume you wanted this, so you probably feel the former."

"*If* I wanted this, it was with good intentions," Rio returns coolly. "I am not your enemy, Silver Kiss."

"And yet, you keep insulting me, Red Rock."

"There is nothing insulting about silver-coated chocolate," the other Alpha bites back. "Those foiled kisses were fucking delicious. Too bad the human world went to shit."

My brother grunts but says nothing more.

"I would like permission to visit," Rio states, abruptly changing the conversation and returning it to business. "I think an in-person discussion regarding current affairs would be best. It'll allow you to evaluate my truths and give me a chance to provide good faith."

"Or you're asking for an opportunity to invade," Onyx fired back. "In which case, I don't recommend it."

Rio smartly ignores my fiery brother and focuses on me instead. He knows I'm the one who can make this decision. Not Onyx.

"Who will accompany you?" I ask him.

"Xavier," he replies. "He can copilot. I'll leave Arlo behind to serve as Sector Prince."

I arch a brow. "No enforcers?"

"I'll happily accept Keegan back, if you're offering."

I narrow my gaze. "He said he's a raider."

Rio smiles. "He's that, too. What's the phrase?" He looks upward, then snaps his fingers. "He's a king of all trades."

"Jack," I correct him, familiar with the idiom he's looking for. "And you just gave me cause to kill him."

Taliana stiffens in my lap, making me instantly regret my words.

"But I won't," I add quickly, kissing her nape as my dragon begins to purr, his need to soothe our startled Omega overriding reason.

If Rio notices, he doesn't comment. Instead, a glimmer of something else darkens his reddish-brown eyes to a deep maroon color. My brother calls him Red Rock because of his ability to create jasper stone. Except it's no ordinary jasper, but magically enhanced rock with lethal properties.

And I spy some of that in his gaze now.

Only, he blinks it away in a flash, his focus on me. "Xavier and I can be there in seven or eight days, with your approval."

"Why seven or eight?" my brother asks.

"I'll need time to ensure that my sector is secure before I leave it unguarded," Riordan tells him flatly. "I don't trust Basalt not to act on an opportunity."

Taliana stiffens again at the mention of *Basalt*. "A week is acceptable," I tell Riordan, wanting to finish this conversation so I can properly soothe my now-trembling Omega. "We'll prepare accommodations for your stay."

"And please let Keegan know I'm coming," he adds.

It's on the tip of my tongue to deny that request. However, the Omega in my arms changes my mind. "I will."

Rio nods. "Then we'll see you soon."

The screen goes dark before I can reply, causing my brother to curse. "Have you lost your mind? We don't know if we can trust him, yet you just gave him approval to enter our waters."

I look at Onyx. "Your bias against Riordan is clouding your judgment."

Both of his eyebrows shoot upward. "You want to talk to me about bias right now?" He glances at Taliana before meeting my gaze again. "Really?"

If Taliana notices, she doesn't show it.

Because her focus is on the floor again.

Which infuriates me on several levels.

"Riordan is our ally," I remind Onyx, my tone underlined with steel. "And he's right to want to meet in person. He knows I can sniff out lies, yet he's willingly allowing himself to be questioned. On our turf, not his own. It's the correct path forward to shore up our alliance against Basalt."

Taliana shudders again, causing my purr to strengthen.

"I'm going to take Taliana back upstairs for breakfast, then we're going on a tour. You're welcome to join us if you want," I offer, aware that I'm being hard on my brother. But he's not exactly going easy on me, either.

He considers me for a moment, realizing the olive branch I'm extending. Or perhaps still worrying that he's lost me entirely to madness. I'm not quite sure.

However, something changes in his features as he looks at Taliana. She's still quivering, despite my dragon's efforts to soothe her. But she's no longer staring at the ground. She's looking at Onyx.

"I think I'll pass on the walk," Onyx says after a beat, his gaze finally returning to me. "But thank you for the offer. We'll talk more later."

Rather than giving me a moment to reply, he ashes out of my office.

I sigh, unsurprised by his response, but also a bit frustrated. We're usually on the same page, our bond literally forged in blood.

Yet we're not on the same page now, not where Taliana is concerned.

"Are you his Second?" she asks slowly, her focus shifting to me as she turns in my lap.

"Would it bother you if I am?" I wonder aloud, studying her features.

"No, but it would explain some things."

"Such as?"

"Your quarters," she says, her eyes seeming to search mine. "Your dominance on that call with the Prince of Jasper Sector."

I hum, nodding. "And what if I'm not a Second, but a prince?"

She swallows. "Are you?"

"I asked how you would feel about that first," I point out, my lips curling a little. "Do positions of power interest you?"

She shakes her head. "No."

"Why not?" I ask, my attention falling to her lips for a brief second before returning to her pretty eyes. "Most Omegas like powerful Alphas."

And if she really is here to ensnare me, then she would be intrigued by my status.

Yet all I see now is concern. "I'm a wolf."

I arch a brow. "Yes, I'm aware."

"I'm not an ideal mate for an Alpha in a position of power, especially in the Drakonian world. I would never be accepted. Definitely not as a prince's mate." She winces on that last part, like she can't even fathom the concept. "You're… you're not a prince, right?"

"Wouldn't it be up to the prince to decide who he feels is an adequate mate?" I ask, avoiding her question.

"Well, I…" She frowns. "Yes, I suppose so. But I would weaken his position."

"Because you're a wolf?" I guess.

She dips her elven-shaped chin in confirmation. "Yes."

"I see." That tour is more imperative now than ever. "Let's revisit this chat after I've shown you around Gold Sector."

Her brow furrows. "So you won't tell me if you're Prince Onyx's Second?"

I smile. "I'm not his Second, Taliana." I kiss her before she can question me further, and ash us back to my bedroom.

She gasps from the sensation, likely having not experienced it much before. Not all Drakonians can teleport, just those of us with unique genetics. I suspect her father lacks the ability. Otherwise, he wouldn't have stayed in Obsidian Sector with his mate and their daughter.

"Wow," she whispers, dazed from the experience.

I press my lips to hers again, then walk us over to the

dining area. "I'll endeavor to impress you again after you eat something," I tell her, setting her in a chair. "Whether it be with my tongue or my ability to ash us to the beach, we'll see, hmm?"

CHAPTER SEVENTEEN

TALIANA

Oros chose the beach.

Yet his words about his *tongue* haunt my every step along the sandy shore. Because I can't stop thinking about his head between my legs.

Which is ridiculous.

He's telling me all about Gold Sector. However, my focus is on his mouth for a reason that has nothing to do with listening to him speak.

Pay attention, I tell myself.

"We lived in the volcano for centuries," he's saying. "The Infection changed that, the disease wiping out almost all the island inhabitants."

He's silent for a moment, like he's quietly mourning the dead.

I idly wonder if he knew any of the humans taken down by the zombielike plague.

But he clears his throat and moves on before I can ask.

He tells me about the destruction, the stench of death lingering in the streets. Then he talks about the rebuilding process, how the Drakonians moved out of the volcano and onto the surface to claim the island as their own.

"And now…" He waves a hand toward the black sand and backdrop of steep cliffs. "This is our home."

Oros continues down the beach, his dark cloak flowing behind him as his golden armor glints in the sun.

I'm similarly dressed color-wise in a long dress that flows to the pebble-like sand beneath my flats.

Everyone eyes me with interest as we pass them, their gazes instantly drawn to my gold adornments—the cuff around my wrist and the necklace he gave me yesterday. Oros doesn't comment on it, just nods hello and flexes his palm against my lower back to keep us moving forward.

He explains the architecture as we walk, telling me how everything is built on the cliffs and hills of the island. "It's steep," he tells me. "But it makes for some beautiful views."

A lot of the foundations were originally created by the humans who once lived here, but the Drakonians expanded on their platforms and bolstered everything with various rocks.

Gold—both yellow and white—is a prominent fixture all around us as we leave the beach for a nearby cobblestone street.

"This is no ordinary gold," he informs me, gesturing to the row of homes before us. "The gold here is enchanted with unique charms that offer protection and prosperity. Which is particularly important on this section of the island."

I'm about to ask why when a woman steps out a few paces ahead, her brown eyes widening at seeing us on the street. My nose twitches, her scent… unexpected. "She's human," I whisper.

"Everyone in this area of the island is," he murmurs as he nods at the brunette. "They're descendants of the mortals who survived over a hundred years ago. There weren't many, but enough to create a small human colony."

He goes on to say how they sometimes save humans on raids and bring them back here.

"It's not common," he says. "But it has happened before."

Then he starts explaining the raids, how they're actually rescue missions involving Omegas.

"We often trade precious metals for Omegas, which is how we've earned our reputation as being in the slave trade. But once the Omegas arrive, they learn the truth."

Oros proceeds to show me that truth as he ashes us to a central street lined with stores and restaurants.

My eyes widen at the sight, the scene before me like something out of a fantasy.

"Obsidian Sector has nothing like this," I whisper. *Neither do the nomad lands*. But that much is probably obvious to him, so I don't mention that last part out loud.

"Want to get a bite to eat?" he asks me. "Maybe a sandwich for a late lunch?"

We've been walking for a long time, making a meal sound like a good idea.

So I nod.

And he takes me to a little café with outdoor seating.

His earlier commentary regarding the island views becomes clearer as I stare down the hill toward the ocean framing the island barrier.

It really is beautiful here, with all the white architecture, blue roofs, and cobblestone streets.

When I say as much out loud, Oros returns to his architecture discussion, saying how it's a tribute to the humans who once lived here. "We maintained a similar appeal, just bolstered it with our enchantments."

It's a bit of a repeat of what he already told me, but I'm so fascinated by it all that I don't mind.

He also reiterates some of his commentary regarding the Omega relocation program as we continue our tour after lunch.

Then he explains how Omegas of all types live here, something he proves when he ashes us to a park area along the Gold Sector coast.

Enchantments dance across my skin as I gawk at the trees embedded in the rocky earth. They are definitely not native to this island, their leaves unlike any I've ever seen. But they instantly appeal to my wolf, my animal eager to explore and take in the unique smells.

"We've created a few different areas in Gold Sector like this, the purpose being to provide an adequate roaming space for the various species that live here."

I'm about to request clarification when a pair of eyes meets mine from inside the forestry area, the yellow orbs instantly making me gasp. *A wolf.*

And not just any wolf, but a petite one with stark white fur.

I frown. "Z-Clan?" I guess, based on the color of her coat. I learned about the different types of wolves while growing up in Obsidian Sector.

Not in a class, but by seeing what kinds of hybrids were created as a result of various experiments.

"Yes. We've acquired a small pack of Z-Clan Omegas," he explains in a soft tone.

He then elaborates on why, saying that Z-Clan Alphas are notoriously brutal, making the Omegas a natural target for rescuing.

"But why do you take on that burden?" I wonder aloud. "I mean, it's admirable. However, I don't understand what you get out of it."

"We're Alphas," he replies. "It's in our nature to cherish Omegas." He palms my cheek as he pulls me toward him. "And Drakonian Alphas are compatible with almost all types of Omegas, too. So I suppose one benefit is potential companionship, but the heart of it is our need to protect."

"The Obsidian Sector Alphas would disagree with you," I mutter. "The Jasper Sector Alphas, too."

"Hmm," he hums, nodding a little. "There are some who believe we should only mate with our own kind. But that's not how things work in Gold Sector. We accept and welcome everyone here."

He kisses me, his mouth reverent against mine. I cling to him, lost to his touch and his words.

I've never been accepted anywhere. But maybe… maybe it really is different here. Maybe I can finally feel like I have a home. A nest. A *mate*.

This all feels like a dream.

A fantasy I never knew existed.

Too good to be true.

Warmth engulfs me as he teleports us somewhere new, his ashing ability foreign and exciting and a bit unnerving. But I trust him not to take me somewhere cruel.

He's been the perfect Alpha thus far.

An amazing potential mate.

"Tomorrow, I'll show you more of the sector," he says against my lips. "And afterward, I'll take you on a proper date."

————

When Oros mentioned taking me on a "proper date," I wasn't sure what he meant.

But now I do.

Because he's escorted me on several outings already, all to different places.

A private restaurant where he introduced me to Greek cuisine.

A hike on one of the smaller islands within Gold Sector territory. That experience was particularly intriguing because I witnessed a Drakonian Alpha kissing his non-dragon mate.

"She's a Grim Wolf," Oros told me.

"From Grim Sector?"

"Yes. She was caught up in some sort of skirmish between Grim Pack and Shade Pack. Alpha Brakish saved her from being dragged off to Darkmoor Sector and brought her here. He was her guardian, and now they're mated."

I blinked, surprised, as I wasn't aware the Grim Sector King allowed anyone in or out of his borders. Nor did I know a lot about the troubles between the two packs, but I knew Grim Sector and Darkmoor Sector bordered one another.

However, what enthralled me most was seeing a dragon with a wolf.

A guardian who had become a mate.

The knowledge stuck with me all night and into the next day when Oros took me to the beach again. Only this time, we didn't stroll. We *swam*.

Which left me in quite a state afterward because we didn't wear clothes.

Not that Oros tried to touch me, though. A fact that's really irritating me now, as it's been five days since he made that comment about his tongue.

And Doctor Taylor's device just finished warning me that I'm on the verge of going into heat. "It could be hours or a few days," Doctor Taylor says as I sit up on the examination table. "It's usually more accurate, but suppressants can alter the results."

I fidget with the gauzy fabric of my black dress and nod, unsure of what to say to that.

"Have you decided how you want to handle your estrus?" she asks as she sets her tablet to the side.

I bite my lower lip and shake my head.

It's a lie.

I want to ask Oros to help me through my heat. However, I can't seem to admit that out loud. Some foolish part of me is worried that he might hear me even though he's not here.

Oh, he escorted me to my appointment with Doctor Taylor. But then he mentioned needing to handle some work.

It likely has something to do with Prince Riordan, as Oros hasn't mentioned him at all since the conversation the other day. And by my calculations, he should be visiting soon.

Does my father know? I wonder now. I haven't spoken to him since we arrived here. *What would he tell me to do about my heat?* I ask myself in the next second.

Which makes me almost groan out loud.

Because talking to my dad about my cycle is not something I want to do.

Besides, I already know what he would recommend—request a mate for my heat.

Does Oros want to be my mate? He says we're courting. He's also kissed me several times. But he hasn't done anything else. Not since our first day together. *Why?*

We've showered together a few times, each experience ending with me feeling far too hot under his soothing hands.

Yet he didn't take me to bed after.

Instead, he fed me, then tucked me in so he could go get some work done.

I tried to stay awake. However, the scent of him and the bed I so badly wanted to nest in always lulled me to sleep.

And the next day, we repeated our wandering, shower, and food.

One day he mixed it up with a shower followed by dinner out. But it ended the same way—with me in his bed alone.

"Taliana?" Doctor Taylor sounds concerned, suggesting I may have missed something she's just said.

"Sorry, I was thinking," I tell her. "What did you ask?"

"If you want a tutorial on the knotting dildos," she replies, making me blanch.

"*What?*"

"Those are the toys I mentioned that some Omegas use to help them through their heats. I can show you—"

"*No,*" I interject, perhaps a little too emphatically. But no. Nope. Not interested. "I..." I shake my head again. "Sorry. It's just, no. I'm not ready for, um, *that.*"

Doctor Taylor stares at me for a moment. "Okay, but your heat—"

"Is imminent," I finish for her on a grumble. "Yeah, I know. I... I'll let you know soon."

She doesn't say anything at first but eventually nods. "All right. I can escort you back to Oros's suite. But please consider talking to him. If you go into heat tonight, he'll need to know your preferences. Otherwise, he won't touch you."

I nearly stumble, her final words having reached me just as I slid off the table. "He won't?"

"He won't," she echoes. "Alphas in Gold Sector value consent. And you can't give consent when you're in the throes of an estrus." There's a sternness to her tone that has me looking at her.

"Have I upset you?" I wonder out loud, confused by her obvious frustration.

"Oh, darling, no," she says with a sigh. "It's just… I'm concerned."

"About my heat?"

She nods. "I know Oros. Unless you explicitly offer permission, he won't see you through your heat. And I'm worried about what it'll do to you… and to him."

I blink. I understand what she means about how it'll impact me. Well, at least, in theory, I do. I've seen other Omegas go into heat. Have witnessed what happens if they don't have an Alpha to see them through it.

Putting an overwhelmed Omega on display behind a cage was one of Basalt's favorite public punishments. Not just for the Omega undergoing estrus, but for the Alphas, too. It caused mass rutting riots—

I shake my head, not wanting to think about what happened on those infamous nights.

My father hid me from most of it, but not all of it.

However, recalling the incidents has me asking, "Will Oros go into a rut?"

Because I… I don't want that for him. At least not in the way I've witnessed before with other Alphas.

"Yes," she says. "But he'll be able to control it. I'm more concerned about how it'll make him feel to watch you suffer, because he'll feel strongly about guarding you through it. However, he won't be able to touch you or help you, and that'll hurt more than any rutting urges."

I frown. "He can control his rut?"

She looks at me. "He's one of the strongest Drakonians I've ever met. If anyone can control his need to rut, it's Oros."

I swallow. I believe her. But part of me doesn't want him to have to control anything. "Do you think… he would knot me if I asked?"

Her eyebrows rise. "Do I think…?" She trails off and clears her throat. "I think you should tell him how you feel, Taliana."

But what if he says no? I want to ask, but don't. It's an insecure question driven by two decades of feeling unworthy.

However, Oros has more than proved this week that my being a wolf doesn't matter to the dragons here. And he wouldn't be courting me if he didn't like me, right?

So why am I nervous? I wonder. *Why can't I just… ask for his knot?*

That Omega from the other day did. She was bold and fearless when requesting his help for her heat.

He turned her down.

Because he has no interest in courting more than one Omega.

He says he wants me. He's spent all this time getting to know me. Maybe because he's my guardian. Maybe because he wants to make me feel comfortable and accepted here.

But hopefully it's mostly because he truly does want me like I want him.

There's only one way to know for sure, I think, swallowing. *I… I have to tell him I want him.*

And I know just how to do it.

By making a nest.

In his bed.

CHAPTER EIGHTEEN
OROS

MY KNOT IS FUCKING KILLING ME.

But rather than being in my suite with Taliana, I'm standing in her father's suite with Rio hovering on a screen between us.

My brother leans against the wall in the corner of the room, his disapproval heavy despite his silence.

When Rio requested a call thirty minutes ago, I assumed it was to discuss his arrival.

Instead, he said he needed to see Keegan first.

"Why?" Onyx demanded.

"I'll explain after I see him" was Rio's reply.

Onyx instantly vetoed that plan. But I allowed it, hence the reason we're here.

But my patience has limits.

His request insinuated that he didn't trust my handling of his friend. And that irritates me.

"Well, you see him," I prompt Rio. "Now tell me why you needed proof of his welfare."

Rio ignores me, his focus on Keegan. "Well?"

"The rumors are true," the Alpha replies.

I arch a brow. "What rumors?"

"That you value your Omegas, regardless of their breed," Rio says, finally looking at me again through the translucent screen. "You were right that I sent Keegan there for a reason, but it's not the reason you suspected."

"So you didn't send him and his daughter here to spy on us?" I ask, trying my best to keep calm despite the flare of anger brewing inside me.

However, before that flare can blaze into an inferno, Keegan says, "Taliana has nothing to do with this."

"She has everything to do with it," Rio corrects, causing that furious flicker to reignite. "But not in the way you think."

"Then tell me what to think," I say through my teeth as fiery energy builds all around me.

I don't bother glancing at Onyx; I know exactly what kind of face he's making right now. The "I told you so" taunt practically radiates off him without him even having to speak.

Or maybe that's just my own internal voice chastising me for falling for Taliana's scent.

It was too good to be true.

She was too good to be true.

"Taliana is about to go into heat, and she needs a mate," Rio says. "So I sent him to you for two reasons. First, I knew her wolf wouldn't be accepted here. And second, I've heard rumors of how your Alphas treat Omegas in Gold Sector."

"Taliana knew neither of those reasons," Keegan interjects. "I prepared her for the worst-case scenario, just like we discussed."

"I know, and that made her the perfect candidate for all of this," Rio replies, glancing at his spy before looking at me again. "I wanted to see how you would treat her. How your *Alphas* treated her."

I glare at him. "So you sent her in here as, what, some kind of test?"

"Yes." There's not even a hint of hesitation or remorse in that one-word response.

"Why?" I demand. "Why do you care how we treat Omegas here? Are you trying to discredit our reputation for cruelty? Because I'll happily prove that reputation as well-earned, right here, right fucking now."

Onyx growls in agreement, a blade appearing in his hand as he ashes to my side.

He's my Second for a reason. My enforcer when I need him. And he'll make an example of Keegan if I allow it. If I *request* it.

"I needed to know before I trusted you with my sister," Rio says, his words so unexpected that my ire momentarily dies.

"Your sister?" I ask, my brow furrowing. "Taliana…?"

"No." He runs his fingers through his hair, his gaze cutting to Keegan again.

Which is really fucking annoying.

"Tell him," Keegan encourages. "You can see what kind of state I'm in—well fed, content, staying in a suite, not a dungeon. While I haven't been permitted to meet with Taliana, I've checked in on her several times without anyone knowing. She's pleased and content."

Rio nods. "I saw her the other day. She's the spitting image of Helena."

Keegan's responding smile is almost sad in nature, not happy. But I can't focus on that so much as the words being exchanged between him and Rio.

When did he check on Taliana? I've been with her every

day. However, I haven't seen him at all, nor has she mentioned him.

"Yes," Keegan murmurs. "Fortunately, Tali is nothing like her mother."

Onyx grunts. "That remains to be seen."

Keegan looks at him. "Helena seduced me with her scent. Used me for my knot. And never had the intention of mating me. All she wanted was to be bred."

"And you expect us to believe your daughter isn't playing a similar game? Particularly after you openly admit to using your daughter as a ploy to enter our waters and spy on our internal processes for an outsider?" My brother twirls a silver blade between his fingers, the picture of calm and deadly. "That alone is grounds for death, *traitor.*"

That has Keegan jumping to his feet. "Hurt me all you want, but Taliana is innocent."

"Is she?" Onyx returns coolly. "Taliana has ensnared my brother in some sort of scented trap, which I already questioned the validity of before. However, now I'm certain it's purposeful and nefarious. And I won't let you or your daughter hurt my prince. My *brother.*"

I blow out a breath, this entire exchange leaving me uneasy.

Valid or not, I don't like discussing Taliana in this manner. I've spent a week with her, gotten to know her more and more each day. And not once have I scented a lie on her.

While it's entirely possible that I'm merely drunk on her perfume and incapable of smelling anything else, I don't think she's here to harm me. She doesn't even know I'm the Gold Sector Prince.

Unless that's a lie, too, and I've misread her entirely.

"I understand," Rio says solemnly. "I feel the same way about my sister. Which is why I asked this of Keegan when he reached out to me with his sanctuary request. I saw the opportunity and seized it. If you want to punish someone, punish me. But I ask that you at least hear me out first."

Onyx is practically vibrating with fury, something I very much understand. But I place my palm on his shoulder to quell him. "Explain," I tell Rio. "Quickly," I add. Because I'm as livid as my brother, perhaps even more so.

Taliana might be innocent in all this, but I don't appreciate being used or tested in this manner.

I asked her a week ago if she wanted a mate, if she was here willingly. And I never coaxed a true response from her.

She was under the impression that taking a mate was her only choice.

Because her father prepared her for this, told her the worst—or at least allowed her to think that way.

No wonder she thought I was going to knot her immediately.

Fuck.

"Basalt is either dead or indisposed," Rio says, his words entirely unexpected and seemingly unrelated to everything we've been discussing. "And I'm fairly certain his Second has aligned Obsidian Sector with the Djinn."

I stare at him. "What the fuck are you talking about?" The alliance with the Djinn isn't a surprise, given recent events, but hearing his thoughts on Basalt is certainly a shock.

"And what the hell does this have to do with your sister?" Onyx adds.

"You mentioned Keegan being my spy the other day and again today," Rio says, ignoring my brother entirely and only focusing on me. "He's more than a spy. He's a fucking chameleon. He could have left with Taliana at any time, but he chose to stay in Obsidian Sector because he sensed something wasn't right. Not just with Helena, but also with Basalt."

Keegan palms the back of his neck and glances out the window, his shoulders rigid. "In nearly two decades there, I never actually saw him. Only Wes, his Second."

"So where's Basalt?" I ask.

"My question precisely," Rio muttered. "Everything is being done in Basalt's name, but it seems Wes is running the show."

"Still not sure how this pertains to your sister," Onyx drawls.

Rio finally looks at him, his expression riddled with irritation. "During the Infected Era, my father and Basalt's father made a blood vow—the Drakonians of Obsidian Sector would stay out of Jasper Sector and Silver Sector if my father agreed to mate his firstborn Omega to an Alpha in Basalt's family line."

I inhale slowly, the mention of the agreement one that brings back a myriad of memories. Of times when arranged matings were common amongst the Drakonians.

Fuck, they're still common. Mostly because that generation of Alphas still exists. We're immortal. Heirs just commonly surpass their fathers in the ranks, our powers naturally strengthening in our offspring when mated to the right Omega.

Hence the purpose of these forced pairings.

Many Alpha fathers have offered me their Omegas, their goals being to align our families and turn their daughters into a princess. They all assumed I wanted a strong heir, too.

They learned quickly that my priorities rest elsewhere.

Thus, I refused all such arrangements.

But now I'm wondering if I fell into one by accident. "Who is your sister?" I ask, my voice lower than before.

He told Taliana to call him *Uncle Rio*. He claimed she wasn't related to him by blood. Said "no" when I asked minutes earlier about their relationship.

Except my stomach is churning with dread, my mind spinning with a thousand ideas. None of them good.

"She's no one you've met, her existence one my family has kept secret for the last twenty-five years. But Basalt's father recently reached out with a missive that made it clear he not only knows of her but is also very aware of her age. And he expects her to appear in Obsidian Sector before her next heat. To wed his youngest son, Alpha Wes."

Keegan's jaw visibly clenches. Though, I doubt this is news to him, given everything that's been revealed thus far in this conversation.

He was sent here to see how Gold Sector handled Omegas.

Used his own daughter as bait.

All to test our Alphas and determine if the "rumors" about our treatment were true. Rumors I'm not entirely sure exist because all I've ever heard about Gold Sector is how cruel we are, how we bargain our precious metals and stones for Omegas, how fearsome we can be when crossed.

Nothing about what actually happens inside our walls.

So either Riordan has another plant—a spy I've yet to unearth—or he was merely guessing. And what a dangerous guess that could have been.

"You want us to help hide your sister," Onyx says slowly, clearly having mentally waltzed down a path similar to the one I just did. Though I hadn't quite reached that conclusion yet, it does feel right.

He sent his chameleon-like spy into my territory to see if we would be a good fit. "What would have happened if we weren't kind?" I ask him, not giving Keegan or Riordan a chance to respond to my brother. "What if we had taken your daughter and raped her like she feared?"

Keegan's eyes narrow, his aggression mounting in a blink. "I would have killed as many Alphas as I could trying to get her back."

"That's one hell of a risk," I tell him, not liking his response in the least. "You would have died trying, and your daughter…" I can't even finish the statement, too disturbed by the realization to say much else. "You literally gambled with her life."

And that infuriates me.

"She deserves better," I growl, no longer keen on this discussion. "She's a diamond. A fucking treasure. And you waltzed her in here, days before her first fucking heat, and just hoped these so-called rumors were true. You're a shit excuse for an Alpha."

Keegan growls low in his throat. "I would die for her."

"Good," I fire back at him. "Because you just fucking might."

I ash out of his quarters, taking Riordan with me since his face is tied to my damn wrist.

But I don't go to Taliana the way my dragon desires. Instead, I teleport to the caves I grew up in, needing a moment to calm the fuck down before I do something I'll regret.

Like kill Taliana's father.

CHAPTER NINETEEN
TALIANA

I sit in the middle of Oros's bed.

Naked.

And evaluate the blankets around me.

We've slept in these sheets the last few nights, making them smell like us. But I need more than just these blankets and sheets.

Hmm.

I crawl out of the pillowy haven to go in search of new linens. It takes a few tries—his closet is *huge*—but I finally locate them in a cabinet near the corner.

Grabbing everything I can find, I carry them through the closet and out into the main suite to set the items on a bench at the foot of the four-poster bed.

My wolf paces eagerly inside me, pleased with this development. We've denned before, but we've never truly nested.

Rubbing my hands together, I suppress a squeal.

Then I get to work.

Strip the bed.

Re-dress the mattress with fresh sheets.

Blankets.

Now… the edges.

I roll the used sheets until they form perfect lines along every side of the massive bed, creating four soft walls to roll between.

And then I grab the pillows to bolster those walls.

Except I don't have enough pillows.

Frowning, I pace around the space, searching for more items I can use to strengthen the edges.

Towels. Only two of those work, the plush fabric meeting my needs. The others don't smell right, so I ignore them. Probably because they don't have enough of Oros's scent.

I find some shirts that remind me of bonfires and add those.

Then I return to the closet to see if there are any more pillows.

None.

Growling, I wander to the living area to investigate the couches there.

No.

I can tell he doesn't sit anywhere in here often.

His office, I decide, almost sprinting for the balcony.

I'm halfway down the stairs when I remember that I'm naked.

Pausing, I listen for anyone nearby.

Hearing nothing, I continue downward and go straight for his desk.

His chair is leather. Not plush. Absolutely unacceptable material for the nest.

The chairs across from it smell more like Voice than Oros, making those definitely not okay. "Ugh," I mutter to myself, frustrated. I don't need that much more, just a few items. Maybe a pillow and a shirt. Or… or…

A cloak!

I run toward his closet, wondering if he has any extras in there. Only to freeze as someone clears a throat from behind me.

My eyes widen.

Then my... my nose twitches.

Sickly sweet.

Omega.

The one Oros called Bella...

I spin toward the familiar blonde, my wolf growling deep inside at the unexpected and unwelcome intrusion in my Alpha's office. *My space. My male. My intended mate.*

"Sorry," she squeaks. "I just saw Onyx downstairs, and he said Prince Oros was out. I... I assumed with you. I... I just... I have..." She blows out a breath and closes her eyes like she's striving for patience or maybe confidence. I don't know.

Because I'm too stuck on something she just said. "Prince... Oros?" The words leave me slowly, the pause unintentional yet entirely necessary. *Prince Oros. That's what she called him, right?*

"Y-yes," she stammers out, then shakes her head and releases a huff. "I'm sorry. I'm not normally this inept. I..." She releases a little snarl that has my wolf instantly on alert. "This is ridiculous. I'm just flustered because I wasn't expecting to see you, and this is the second time I've fucked up."

Her eyes widen, and she covers her mouth like she can't believe she just spoke those words.

"Sorry," she mumbles behind her hand. "Gods, you must think I'm not only inconsiderate but an idiot, too!" Her cheeks turn a bright pink, making me frown.

"Why would it matter what I think?" I ask her. *I'm just a*

wolf, I nearly add. Meanwhile, she's a gorgeous dragon. Maybe a bit… odd. But stunning nonetheless.

"Because you're Prince Oros's chosen Omega," she says reverently. "My future princess." Her eyes widen. "Oh, crap, I should have curtsied." She proceeds to do so, and I realize it's as awkward as my own curtsying abilities.

I blink at her, waiting for her to stop.

She doesn't.

I look around, trying to figure out what the heck she's doing.

Yet all she does is hold that damn position and cast her eyes downward.

"Please forgive me, Your Future Highness," she whispers.

Now I… I just gape at her. "*Stop*," I say, and it comes out a bit shrill.

Which makes the female jump backward. "I'm sorry. I… I didn't mean to… *Fuck*. I mean damn. I mean, *crap*…" Her eyes widen, and if she didn't look so terrified, I may have laughed at her rush of words. "You're going to have me exiled, aren't you?"

"What? No! Of course not. Why the hell would I do that?" I ask, astounded by her claim. "I don't have that kind of power, nor would I ever do that to anyone. Especially not an Omega."

Her shoulders fall, and her bottom lip begins to tremble. "Really? Because I… I stupidly propositioned your Alpha. But I didn't know. I swear I didn't. Prince Oros has always been kind to me, and I… I like him. But not like that. Well, yes, like that." She grabs her head. "Oh, damn it, Bella, stop yapping!"

A laugh bubbles out of me on impulse, one I don't mean to voice or display, but I can't help it.

This is the strangest conversation I've ever had.

And I no longer feel like challenging this woman. All I want to do is hug her.

Because I understand her. That fear. That need to apologize. That desire to survive.

Her blue eyes are wide as she stares at me, her terror somewhat quelling my giggles. I'm not actually amused at all; it's just a nervous response.

But after a beat, she joins me. And suddenly we're both simply… *laughing*.

It's insanity. Yet it feels good. Like an emotional explosion that simply needed to happen.

At least until I realize the real reason I can't stop giggling. It's because the alternative is crying. Or losing my damn mind.

Prince Oros.

I knew he held a high position. His suite. The call with Riordan. The way everyone stared reverently at him in the kingdom.

Deep down, I suspected this. I even asked him about it. But he sidestepped his response, saying we would return to the discussion later.

Only, we never did.

And now I know why.

Oros is the Gold Sector Prince.

Oh, Gods…

"Why do you think I'm your future princess?" I ask after a beat of silence, my focus returning to Bella.

"Because Prince Oros is formally courting you," she replies, a little frown marring her porcelain-like forehead. "He's taken you all over the sector and adorned you with gold." She looks pointedly at my necklace and my cuff. "You're wearing his symbol."

I glance down at the bracelet and the fiery lotus

embedded in the metal. I never asked him what it meant, but I noticed it when I first put it on. "This," I whisper.

"Yes."

I meet her gaze again and note the confusion in her expression. "I didn't realize he was a prince," I tell her. "I... I suspected he might be, but he never..." I trail off, not wanting to confide more than I already have. "Anyway, I... I can let him know you stopped by?"

She shakes her head. "No. I just needed to drop this file off from the Kuanos Quarter," she says, digging in her bag and pulling out a folder. "It's a request for supplies."

"Oh. So you're... you help Oros?"

"Um, not really, no. I help Kuanos Quarter. It's the human village. I think you visited the other day?"

I nod. "He didn't tell me the name but explained that they're descendants of the Infection survivors."

She smiles. "Yes. They have some fun tales, not of that period, but other mythology stories. You should visit again. I'm sure they would love to have you over for coffee sometime." Her eyes widen like she can't believe she just said that. "I mean, if you... if you want. I know you'll be... busy."

"You don't have to worry about what you say to me," I tell her, hating that she's so nervous.

Because I know how that feels. As a wolf Omega, none of the dragons wanted to talk to me. They saw me as lower than them. Unworthy. A burden, not a being.

"I like talking to you," I add, smiling a little. "It's... refreshing."

"Refreshing?" she repeats.

"Yeah. It's different. New. Good, I think? I don't know. But now I'm the one rambling." I grin again. "What's your name?" Oros called her *Bella*, so I've been doing the same.

But I really don't want to use Oros's endearment for her. Just thinking about him calling her—

"Bella," she says, interrupting my thoughts and making me frown.

"Bella," I repeat, unable to hide my confusion.

"It's short for Isabella," she murmurs, blushing a little. "But I prefer to go by Bella. Or Bell, if you like."

My lashes flutter. "Oh." *Ohhh*. "It's not... I mean, right. Okay. I've only ever heard *bella* as an endearment."

Her eyes widen. "*Bella* is an endearment in your homeland?"

I nod, then frown. "Well. Kind of. Yes." I don't really want to explain that the Alphas used it interchangeably to call for Omegas there. "Um, I'm Taliana," I tell her instead of elaborating on Obsidian Sector practices. "But you can call me Tali."

That last part just sort of falls off my tongue. I haven't told Oros my nickname. But that's because I rather like the way "Taliana" sounds when he voices it.

As well as "printesa mea."

I shiver just thinking about it.

"Tali," Isabella—whom I'm definitely calling *Bell*, not *Bella*—repeats.

"Yes." I smile. "And I think 'Bell' is beautiful, by the way."

Her lips curl as well. "Thank you." She steps forward to place the envelope on Oros's desk. "And thank you for not hating me. I know it's probably hard, given my past with Oros and all that."

I stare at her. "But that was before I met him." Not to mention the fact that I have no right to feel anything about his former or current lovers.

Gods, he's a prince...

He also said he only wants one Omega, another part of me whispers. *He's yours and only yours.*

Except he hasn't tried to do more than kiss me all week.

"It doesn't matter," Bell says, grabbing my attention once more. "You have every right to feel possessive."

My wolf huffs with approval inside. Or maybe it's agreement. I'm not sure.

"But you should know that the second I heard him purr, I knew he wasn't mine," Bell goes on. "It's such a strange thing to say, so I'm sure you find it odd as well. But it gave me a unique sense of closure the other day when he purred for you. The sound didn't soothe me at all."

"You don't like his purr?" I ask, confused because I love that sound. It's one of my favorites despite being new.

"It's not that I dislike it, but that purr is only for you." She smiles. "He never purred for me. Not once. He also barely ever kissed me. But with you…" She gives a dreamy sigh. "I only saw a glimpse of you both on the balcony, but it was all I needed to witness to know that he's yours."

I swallow, wishing I shared her confidence.

"Well, anyway, I should go. And you…" She glances over me. "I assume you were in the middle of something important."

Frowning, I look down.

And remember that I'm naked.

"Oh. I…"

"It's fine," she says, waving it away. "I know the signs of an oncoming heat. And besides, we're all shifters here." She starts to leave, then pauses. "Do you need anything? Blankets? Water? Food?"

"Um." My frown seems to deepen. "No, I think I'm okay. But thank you." All I really need is Oros, wherever he is. I glance at the balcony platform, almost hoping he'll appear.

He doesn't.

"If you change your mind…" Bell trails off as she jots something down on a paper that she pulled from her purse. "That's how you reach me."

"Oh, thank you." I don't bother telling her that I have no idea how this number works. I'll either figure it out or ask Oros. *Assuming he comes back.*

Bell mentioned being told that he wasn't here.

So where is he?

I don't ask Bell. Instead, I say goodbye, then head back up the stairs to his suite.

Why isn't he here? I wonder, looking at the nest I've created and experiencing an unexpected sense of dread. I'm not sure where it comes from, maybe my own insecurities.

But I suddenly feel like something is very wrong. To the point that my insides begin to churn.

I walk over to the nest and crawl inside, my limbs beginning to shake.

Deep breaths, Tali, I tell myself. But all that does is worsen the sensation.

I'm clearly panicking.

It's ridiculous.

I just need to be patient.

Wait for Oros.

Also known as the Gold Sector Prince.

CHAPTER TWENTY
OROS

A Few Minutes Earlier

"You're right to be pissed," Riordan says, reminding me that I never hung up our call.

He's been watching me pace for the better part of ten minutes.

I go to hang up on him when he adds, "If you care about your Omega at all, you'll let Keegan live."

My eyebrow lifts at that. "My caring about her is why I want to fucking kill him." The bastard threw his daughter into my Royal Court without a single care as to what we might have done to her. He didn't deserve to breathe.

"Keegan loves his daughter," Riordan tells me.

I snort. "He has a fucked-up way of showing it."

"He knew she would be safe in Gold Sector."

"Based on these supposed rumors you've heard," I drawl. "Yeah, I got that part."

"No. Based on his own observations," Riordan replies, a hint of steel coming through his tone. "He's a Stealth Royal, Oros."

I stop walking. "That's a myth." Stealth Royals are the beings Drakonians tell whelps about to make them behave. *Don't misbehave or the Stealth Royals will see you and tell everyone what you did.*

A ridiculous tale about Drakonians who can vanish into thin air, then come and go at will. Basically like spirits.

"It's not," Riordan tells me. "It's a rare gift, one Keegan possesses. He can prove it to you."

I stare at him. "By what? Disappearing? Because I can do that, too." I do it all the time when I ash to another location.

"He visited Gold Sector several times before deciding to take Tali there," Riordan says, ignoring what I said. "And before you ask, no, he didn't bring her with him. She doesn't possess the same talents."

I fold my arms. "So you're saying he's been spying on my sector for a while now?"

"I'm saying he visited various Drakonian territories, and a few wolf packs, too, in order to decide where to take his daughter. He's been hunting for an ideal location for nearly five years."

My jaw ticks. "If he was in Gold Sector, I would have sensed him."

"Except you didn't," he replies. "I know it's hard to believe, but as I said, he can prove it. He's a Stealth Royal."

I consider Riordan for a long moment. "All right. Let's say I agree to believe in this myth. Why did he need to test us with his daughter?"

"It was never a test for him, Oros. It was a test for me."

I narrow my gaze. "Elaborate."

He sighs and runs a hand over his tight braids, the tattoos along his scalp seeming to tense in response.

"Since Jasper Sector would never accept his daughter

—that part we both know is true—I told him to go to you and to report back to me on the results. He could have done it in stealth mode, but I opted to speak to him in front of you. Because I wanted you to know."

"How kind of you," I drawl, unable to hide my sarcasm.

His hand drops to his side. "Look, I meant it when I said I wanted to visit to firm up our alliance. What I didn't add is that I would like to bring my sister, too. I needed to hear Keegan's report before I could even begin to ask."

"And now you want to request a favor," I conclude for him. "After thoroughly pissing me off."

"Yes."

I huff a humorless laugh. "You have some nerve."

"If an Omega under your care was promised to a tyrant, what would you do?" he demands. "Now imagine that Omega is your own flesh and blood."

"Decline the request," I suggest. That's what I would do in his position, anyway.

"I fully intend to," he returns without hesitation. "But my sister has it in her mind that she should be a martyr and give herself up. Which is why I need somewhere safe to hold her until this problem is resolved."

My eyebrows lift. "You mean you want to imprison her somewhere so she doesn't fulfill the blood vow your family engaged in with Basalt's father."

"Yes." He doesn't elaborate, just gives me a hard stare like that's somehow going to convince me to cooperate.

I close my eyes and dig deep for the energy I seem to have displaced. All I want to do is flame everything around me. Which won't do much since the entire cave is full of singed black rock.

"My sister is twenty-five, and she's a little hellion princess who won't listen to reason," Riordan confides softly, obviously realizing he'll have to try a bit harder to convince me.

I tell him without words that it's not enough by resuming my pacing.

"I won't let her waltz into Wes's lair. It's clearly a trap. And I'm fairly certain he's the one who penned the letter, not his father. I'm not even sure if his father is still alive; no one has seen him in decades. Regardless, I can't go confront Wes because my sister will no doubt follow, and then she'll sacrifice herself for me."

"Sounds like you have a loyal sister," I mutter, though his commentary about Wes has me paying attention a bit more.

"She's a brat, but she has a beautiful soul, and I refuse to let Wes have her. However, I need to figure out how he learned of her existence, and I want to know where he's keeping Basalt. Because Basalt might be the only one who can stop this nonsense. Assuming he's even alive."

I pause my walking once more and look at the screen that's been following my every step. "How long have you suspected that Basalt isn't truly in charge?"

"Since the day Keegan arrived in Obsidian Sector," he informs me. "Wes is the one who greeted him, which isn't necessarily a red flag, but he made the decision to grant Keegan entry. It would be akin to Xavier letting your brother enter my sector without talking to me."

I nod, agreeing with that assessment. "Maybe Basalt and Wes have a unique agreement. They're brothers, after all."

Although, I certainly don't have that power dynamic with Onyx.

Most Alphas and Seconds maintain similar power structures whereby the Second only stands in when the prince requests it. But that doesn't mean a deviation of power is impossible. So perhaps Basalt and Wes just operate differently.

"I considered that," Rio says. "That's one of the reasons Keegan offered to poke around. But he couldn't find Basalt anywhere."

"Which is a feat, considering he's supposedly a Stealth Royal," I say, still unable to mask my sarcasm.

But if Riordan notices it, he doesn't comment. Instead, he just says, "Yes." Then he continues with, "Keegan stayed there until weeks before Taliana's first heat and never once found even an inkling of Basalt's presence."

"And no one in Obsidian Sector is aware of this?" I wonder aloud, becoming a little too intrigued by this outlandish tale.

"The Drakonians of Obsidian Sector are too busy trying to survive to notice that the leader they all fear has been missing for years," Riordan growls out.

"Seems like a convenient excuse," I tell him.

His eyes narrow. "Has Taliana told you what happens to disobedient Omegas in Obsidian Sector? How they're put in cages during the initial phase of their estrus and left on display?"

My teeth gnash together as I look at him again.

"It induces a rut," he goes on. "And any Alphas with claims on those Omegas, or relations to them, are forced to watch as they're freed and ripped apart."

"Why are you telling me this?" I demand, my stomach churning at the violent visual his words just painted.

"Because that's only one of the methods used to control the beings of Obsidian Sector. So no, it's not *convenient* at all. Everyone there is just trying to survive. Keegan originally wanted to help Helena, but she was too indoctrinated to save. So he stayed to gather intelligence, then fled with Taliana before it was too late."

"And took her to the nomad lands," I say, aware of that part. "Then apparently spied on other sectors and eventually brought her here."

"Yes. But only after he knew it would be safe for her. However, he wasn't kidding when he said he would have died fighting for her. That Alpha loves his daughter. Which is why he'll understand if you want to kill him for what you think he's done. I doubt he'll even try to stop you."

Onyx materializes beside me before I can reply to that. "I thought I might find you…" My brother trails off when he realizes I'm still talking to Riordan. "Seriously, I've seen enough of your face this week to last me a damn decade."

"I understand," Riordan says solemnly. "The competition is quite fierce, and you need some time to recover your ego."

"Oh, fuck you, Red Rock. My ego is just fine."

"Hmm," he hums. "Then you're questioning your sexuality? Are you feeling a bit too attracted to me, Silver Kiss?"

Onyx rolls his eyes. "I will not deign to respond to that." He looks at me. "I came to warn you that your Omega knows you're a prince."

I take a step back, my eyes widening. "What? How?"

"Bella told her, but not on purpose. She assumed she knew."

"Why the fuck was she talking to Bella?" I demand.

"She went up to drop something off in your office and ran into Taliana. I'd told her you weren't around. It's my fault she was there." He sounds contrite, causing me to narrow my gaze.

"Did you overhear the conversation?"

"Only the end," he mutters. "I realized what I'd done by letting her up there—while Taliana is in your suite— and went to rectify the situation. But they were already deep in their discussion when I got there. So I... I just waited outside the door to escort Bella back down."

I sigh. "What were they discussing?"

"Kuanos Quarter, when I arrived. Bella was suggesting that Taliana visit to hear some of the old mythology tales." His lips twitch. "Your Omega was intrigued."

"And?" I press.

"And the two exchanged some words about their names—apparently, Taliana thought 'Bella' was an endearment. Their conversation ended shortly after that."

My brow furrows. "Yet Bella told her I'm a prince?"

"Yes. When Bella found me waiting in the hall for her, she asked me why you hadn't told her." He winces. "She doesn't approve."

I refrain from the urge to growl.

Then the sound of a pen scribbling across paper drags my attention to the screen where Riordan is making a show of writing something down. "What the hell are you doing?"

He glances up from his task. "Oh, I'm just taking notes on what not to do when I find my future Omega. Top of the list is *Don't lie about who I am*."

This time, my growl escapes me. "You're an asshole."

"I am," he agrees, smirking. "One who still plans to visit you in twenty-four hours. And I'm bringing my sister with me."

My gaze widens. "I haven't agreed to take her yet."

"I know. So consider this a meet and greet. Once you see what I'm dealing with, you'll happily lock her up in a cell while I go handle Wes and track down Basalt."

"That is not what we agreed to," I tell him.

"You know, you're—"

Static sounds.

"Breaking up. I—"

More static.

I glare at the glitching screen.

"See you tomorrow."

The call cuts short.

My jaw begins to ache from clenching it so tightly. "I don't have time to deal with him."

"I'll handle it," Onyx offers. "Your Omega needs you."

I blink, then look at him. "That almost sounds like you approve."

"Maybe I do."

My eyebrows lift. "Since when?"

"Since it became clear that she's innocent."

"Not even an hour ago, you stated otherwise," I remind him, referring to what he said in Keegan's room.

He shrugs. "A lot can change in sixty minutes."

"And what changed your mind?"

"Hearing her talking to Bella," he replies.

"About Kuanos Quarter?" I ask, confused as hell.

"No. It was… her tone." He frowns. "I can't explain it. There was just a genuine curiosity in her voice that can't be faked. I also spent a few extra minutes threatening Keegan after you left, and all he asked was that we spare his daughter." He pauses, then adds, "I don't need to be a lie detector to know he meant it."

"So you don't think she knew about any of this," I say, confirming where my brother stands.

"No, and I think you already know she didn't," he tells me. "Her scent might have been manufactured to attract you, but she's not trying to ensnare you. Hell, she didn't even know you were the Gold Sector Prince until tonight."

"The only one playing tricks here appears to be Riordan," I growl.

"Which I've already said I'll handle," my brother

reiterates. "So go to your nesting Omega and let me play my role as Second."

His words have my heart skipping a beat. "She's nesting?"

"That's what Bella told me, yes. Hence the reason I said your Omega needs—"

I've already ashed before he can finish speaking, my mind on Taliana nesting. *In my suite.*

Her scent hits me the moment I materialize beside my bed.

Then the sight of her nearly brings me to my knees.

She's waiting on her knees in the center of a pillowed safe haven made of familiar sheets and clothes.

A nest.

"Oros," she breathes, her starry eyes widening at the sight of me. "You're here."

"I'm here," I tell her, already unclasping my cloak to let it float to the ground in my wake. "And you are *very* naked."

CHAPTER TWENTY-ONE
TALIANA

My cheeks warm at Oros's obvious approval, his eyes roaming over me with stark interest as he prowls toward the bed. "I want you to knot me," I blurt out, causing his gaze to snap up to mine.

I wince.

"That… that didn't come out…" I bite my tongue, irritated at my faltering. I want to be confident. Sexy. *Seductive*. Not babbling. Yet I also don't want to lose my nerve. Which means it's imperative that I say everything I want to say as fast as possible. "You're the Gold Sector Prince."

He unfastens the top button of his black pants. His torso is already bare, thanks to his penchant for only wearing cloaks.

I very much like his wardrobe choices.

"Yes, I am," he confirms. "Does that bother you?"

I considered that very question while sitting in my nest. And I realized there was really only one aspect that upset me. "Why didn't you tell me?"

Oros holds my gaze as he replies, "Because I wanted you to trust me."

"By omitting the truth?" I ask, frowning. "That seems like a poor way to gain trust."

He nods. "You're right. And I almost told you my identity when you asked if I was Onyx's Second. But then you told me you could never be worthy of a prince, and my priorities shifted."

My frown deepens. "What do you mean? What priorities?"

"It became imperative to prove to you that you're more than worthy of being a prince's mate." He sits on the bench rather than the bed and draws up one of his knees. "I also needed to determine your motives for desiring me."

"My motives?" I stare at him. "My father brought me here to find a mate. What other motives could I have?"

"Your scent is like a drug to me," he replies. "And from what your father has told me, your mother's was a drug to him, too."

My mother? I swallow, not liking the thought of me being anything like her. "I'm not Helena. She used my father to procreate, then ran off to seduce another Alpha."

Some Omegas were bred to do that, their minds conditioned to accept their fates.

But my mother—*Helena*—liked her role. She wielded her sexuality like a weapon. And I would have been just like her had I been born with the right combination of genetics.

Because she would have taken me under her wing and trained me in her shadow.

Alas, I'm all wolf.

My mother may be a mixed breed, but she can at least shift into a dragon.

However, it's her unique genetic blend that allows her to seduce different types of male shifters.

Shifters like my father, I think.

"You thought I meant to entrap you," I realize out loud, my gaze on Oros. "That's why you questioned my motives. But I had no idea you were the prince when we first met. And I'm not one of the Omega seductresses. I was never trained in that art… because of my wolf."

I elaborate a bit, telling him about Helena's role in Obsidian Sector and how I thankfully never qualified to learn from her.

Which leads me to reiterating that I am *not* her.

And finally admitting, "I don't want your knot because you're a prince. I… I like you." I pause for a beat, swallowing. Then finish what I need to say. "I'm close to going into heat, and I know you need my consent. Please know that you have it. If… if you want to help me through my estrus, I would like that."

He's silent for a beat, his gaze evaluating. "So you're not cross with me?"

My brow furrows. "For not telling me about being a prince?"

He nods.

"I… I'm disappointed that you couldn't trust me. It hurts. But I had some time to think about it before you returned, and, well, I understand why you didn't tell me," I admit. "You made me think you're that Rumpelstiltskin guy instead."

His eyes widen, then he releases a low laugh, one that does funny things to my insides. "Because I gave you gold?"

"To impress the court, or the prince, or whoever," I say. "Yes."

He chuckles again. "I guess I am your Rumpelstiltskin,

then, hmm?" He glances down at my nest, then back up at me. "I suppose I do want your firstborn," he goes on, causing my heart to skip a beat. "Because I want to create that firstborn with you. When you're ready."

My breath catches in my throat. "An heir."

"*Our* heir," he murmurs, his head canting to the side and causing some of his long blond hair to fall across his face. "I'm not really Rumpelstiltskin, remember? The gold was a gift without strings. A token of my affection. But I will eventually want a whelp. With you."

I swallow. "Okay."

"Okay?" he echoes. "Okay, as in you'll want a whelp, too?"

I nod, my lips curling a little. "Does that mean you want to knot me?"

His golden irises flicker with fire. "Oh, I've wanted to knot you since the moment we met in that royal chamber, little diamond."

I'm confused for a moment, not following what he means.

Until it dawns on me…

"You were the gold dragon."

"I was the gold dragon," he confirms, smiling. "My brother, Onyx, did all the talking. That's how we usually run our introduction sessions. My sense of smell is stronger in dragon form. And one of my skills is the art of sniffing out lies."

He moves on the bench, angling himself toward me a little more.

"Your scent overwhelms me, making me question my ability. But I don't think you're here to ensnare me, even though you quite clearly have." His gaze dances across the nest. "And I really want to crawl in there with you, printesa mea. However, I need to know what your rules are."

"Rules?" I parrot back to him, my voice a little breathless at the thought of him finally joining me in my nest.

Part of me realizes I just made it, yet I feel like I've been waiting for this moment for a very long time.

"Knotting you may encourage you to go into heat," he tells me. "Are you okay with that? Do you feel ready?"

I bite my lip. Am I ready? No. Probably not. But… "I trust you to help me," I reply. "So, because of that, I think I'm ready. I just don't really know what to expect. I mean, I've seen others…" I don't finish the statement because I don't want to think about anyone else.

I only want to think about Oros.

About this.

About *us*.

"There's a part of me that's nervous," I admit. "But I'm also… excited." Because I want to feel his tongue again. His hands. His mouth. And I want to explore him, too.

To finally touch his knot.

I've seen it in the shower. Saw it while naked on the beach. But I haven't been able to stroke him. To squeeze him. To *taste* him.

I want all those things and more.

"I'll check in with you the entire time," he says, his eyes holding mine.

"Okay," I whisper. I know it's going to hurt. I've heard the screams. But I hope he'll also make me feel good. Like he did the other day.

"Do you want me to use protection?"

My brow crinkles. "Protection?"

"It's a pill," he says. "One that'll ensure we don't create a baby. During your heat, I mean."

"Oh. I… I didn't know that was possible."

He smiles. "I'm going to assume there are a few things you don't know, little diamond. Things I can't wait to teach you." His smile dims a bit. "But I need to know how you feel about procreating first."

"I… I don't know. I just assumed…"

"That it would be required when you took a mate?" he guesses.

I nod.

"Hmm, that tells me your answer, then," he says softly. "I'll use protection. We still need time to develop our bond anyway. And honestly, I don't think I want to share you just yet."

"Sh-share me?" My stomach flips at the notion. "I thought—"

"Share your attention with our little heir," he interjects, his words instantly soothing me.

Because that was not what I assumed he meant at all.

"Yet another reason to take the pill—you still need time to understand how things work here." He reaches forward to catch my hand and gives it a gentle squeeze.

I weave my fingers through his, desperate to hold on to him. Or maybe to drag him into the nest.

Gods, it feels like there's an ocean between us, his body still seated on the bench while I kneel in the middle of his bed.

"Next question," he says, his thumb drawing a path along my hand. "Can I claim you?"

The inquiry steals my breath, making it impossible to answer.

"I know it's fast," he goes on, his golden irises captivating me right along with his smooth tones. "You don't have to claim me back, printesa mea. I'm okay with extending our courtship, but I need to know if I'm allowed to bite you. It'll help me decide how much control I need to assert over my dragon."

I shiver at the thought of him biting me. I always assumed my claiming would be violent. Cruel. *Unwilling.*

But Oros is unexpectedly gentle about it, asking for permission, telling me how he feels, and trying to ascertain my needs before acting.

"I feel like I'm living in a dream," I admit, my gaze searching his. "Why are you so kind?"

His lips curl. "Oh, I'm not kind, little diamond. I'm thorough. Now tell me how you feel about biting."

"I… I'm okay with biting."

"Good." His thumb draws another shape against my skin. "And how do you feel about me being in charge of your heat?"

My stomach clenches at the thought of relying on him while I'm in estrus. "I want you to knot me," I tell him again, this time in a more sultry voice. It's not perfect, but I see the way his pupils dilate in response to my words.

"I know, little diamond. But how do you feel about me making decisions for you while you're lost to your heat?"

I swallow. "I trust you to make decisions on my behalf."

He grins again, and there's something decidedly wicked about that look. "That's what I needed to hear. Now there's just one question left."

My nipples tighten at the promise in his words. "What is it?" I ask, my voice a breath of expectation.

His sinful gaze dances over me before coming up to rest on my lips. "Taliana, may I enter your nest?"

CHAPTER TWENTY-TWO
OROS

Fuck, Taliana is beautiful.

Naked.

Aroused.

Staring at me with a look of wild wonder in her pretty eyes.

I want to leap forward and devour her. It's taken serious restraint this week to keep my hands to myself.

Oh, I've indulged in the urge to stroke her in the shower. Given in to the need to claim her mouth. To fuck her with my tongue.

But I've held back otherwise.

Provided her with the time she needed to acclimate to how things work here.

Seduced her with my *kindness*, as she called it.

All under the guise of courtship.

However, I've known from the beginning that I wanted this Omega. I questioned certain aspects, debated her intentions, but deep down, I knew the truth.

This Omega is meant to be mine.

I'd rejected all those mating requests for a reason—

none of them had appealed to me. Not like this. Not like *Taliana*.

Her full mouth curves into an enticing smile as she says, "Please enter *our* nest, Prince Oros."

"Hmm," I hum, rather liking that formal title on her tempting lips. "If you want to address me as your prince in the bedroom, I'll allow it," I decide as I stand. "But I'm only Oros in public."

Her brow furrows. "Shouldn't it be the opposite?"

I tug the zipper down on my pants, causing her focus to instantly jump to my groin. There's no way in Hades that I'm getting in her—*our*—nest with my clothes on.

"If you're to be my mate, then you'll be my equal. And I want everyone to be clear on that, which means you'll need to refer to me as Oros around them."

I kick off my shoes, socks, and pants, leaving me naked before her.

"You'll never bow to me, Taliana," I go on, sliding onto the bed. "At least, you'll never bow where anyone can see."

I start crawling toward her, my gaze holding hers the entire time.

"But I will absolutely make you bend in here," I say as I grab her nape and go to my knees before her on the bed. "You can call me *prince* while I master you. *Your Highness* and *Alpha* work, too." I lean down to nip at her bottom lip. "You can even call me *God*."

She inhales, causing her chest to meet mine.

"I'm going to master you now, Omega," I warn her.

Her pupils blow wide, her sweet scent permeating the air.

It's all the invitation I need to *claim*.

Only, I don't bite her the way my dragon desires. I take her mouth instead and force her to accept my tongue.

She grabs my shoulders, holding on while I consume her with my cravings. My passion. My pent-up *need*.

Fuck, she tastes like decadent sin. A temptation I can't refuse. A future I long to embrace.

Her nails dig into my skin like she's trying to anchor herself to me. I tighten my grip on her nape, my opposite hand going to her hip.

She melts against me, letting me guide her down to the mattress. "My precious little diamond," I say against her mouth. "The perfect mate for my possessive and dominant beast."

Her breasts pillow my chest as I settle on top of her, my cock instantly finding her wet heat.

She spreads her legs in warm welcome, her body automatically submitting to mine. But I know better than to thrust into her.

Taliana needs my mouth. My touch. My *expertise*.

I nibble on her plump lower lip as my hand slides up to palm her breast. She arches into me on a moan, her body seeming to burn beneath me.

So hot. So primed. So mine.

I tweak her nipple, and she whimpers against my mouth in response, my name escaping her on a breath.

"*Prince* Oros," I remind her. "Or Alpha." My knot throbs just thinking about those words on her lips.

She obliges me with a moaned "*Alpha*" in response.

"Such a good fucking Omega," I praise her. Then I kiss her again until she's panting and writhing beneath me, her peak exceptionally stiff beneath my fingertips. "Don't move," I demand as I leave her mouth for her breast.

"*My prince*," she screams as I take her hard nipple between my teeth and bite down.

A growl rumbles in my chest, my dragon pleased with

my choice. But he wants more. Another bite. This time hard enough to break the skin.

However, I shove him down.

I want to make this last.

To taste my Omega properly. Tease her. Prepare her for my knot. Then fuck her into oblivion.

I switch to her other breast, my dragon humming in approval as our Omega writhes beneath us. Flames, she's so fucking perfect. The way she moves. The way she claws at my shoulders. The way she continues to moan.

Gods, I want her more than I've ever desired anything or anyone.

"I still want to pierce you," I tell her. "Will you let me pierce you with my gold, Taliana?"

She lifts her head, her eyes finding mine. "Will it hurt?"

"Yes. But I'll make you feel good, printesa mea. I promise."

She shudders and bites her lip, then nods. "Okay."

My dick pulses in response to her acceptance. "Gods, you're incredible." I sink my teeth into her nipple, giving her a little pinch before I lave the pain away. "I'll pierce you during your heat while my knot is so deep inside you that your pleasure masks most of the pain."

Her tight form shivers again, the sensation one I feel against my own skin.

And a fresh wave of slick perfumes the air.

"Mmm, you like that, don't you?" I say, kissing a path downward to taste the sweetness between her thighs. "Fuck, little diamond, you're so wet you're glistening."

I part her folds with my fingers, then go straight for her clit.

The little nub pulsates against my tongue, her ecstasy a flavor I will never tire of. She's in my skin. My heart. My fucking soul. And I want to keep her there for eternity.

Fires, I want to claim her here…

My dragon is practically beating at my chest, demanding that I lay claim to her most intimate part.

But I tame him with a growl, telling him to be patient.

Because I want to knot her first.

Fuck her so good that she forgets her own name. *Then* I'll properly brand her.

"Maybe I'll pierce you here, too," I murmur.

"*Alpha,*" Taliana groans in response, more dampness pooling in her center.

Dampness I quickly shove back into her with my fingers.

She jolts at the intrusion, her tight sheath unaccustomed to such sensation. But I quickly introduce her to the pleasure of being full.

All while tormenting her with my tongue.

"Are you going to be a good little Omega and come for me?" I ask against her hot flesh.

She quivers in response, goose bumps pebbling sweetly down her thighs.

I hum in approval, the vibration right against her weeping center. Her back arches in response, an unintelligible word escaping her as her slick cunt convulses around my fingers. I add a third and curl them in just the right way to make her explode on a scream.

It's a fucking delicious sound, one I want to hear again as I introduce her to my cock.

I crawl back up her panting form to reach her mouth, my tongue instantly seeking hers as I force her to taste her pleasure while she continues to come against my hand.

"Hold on to that sensation, printesa mea," I tell her softly. "Remember how good you feel right now and know that it's only the beginning of what I can do to you."

Her lashes flutter open, her cheeks a beautiful shade of pink. There's a little note of confusion in her features, like she's not sure what I'm saying.

I don't elaborate.

I don't explain.

I just pull my fingers away from her sweet pussy and grab my shaft to give it a stroke.

"My palm is so fucking wet from you, Taliana," I inform her with a groan. "Flames, just a single pump of my fist has me soaked from tip to hilt."

A little more awareness enters her features, her gaze flickering downward.

I don't hide what I'm doing, instead lifting my hips so she can watch me angle my cock toward her weeping heat.

I look so big compared to her, but I know she can take me. Fuck, she was built for me. Not just with her scent, but with her sexy little body, too.

"Grab my shoulders," I demand. "Hold on to me and don't be afraid to scream. I know this is going to hurt. But I'll make it up to you, printesa mea."

She releases a little sound of protest, one I don't think she meant to let escape. However, her hands obey me, her nails digging into my skin on instinct.

Her pretty eyes are focused on where my head meets her entrance, her nostrils flaring as I begin to push forward.

Taliana's lips part on a squeak that turns into a pant, but my perfect little Omega accepts my girth like she was made to. "You're taking me so fucking well, sweet diamond," I praise her, my voice deeper as I fight the urge to thrust all the way into her.

"Oh!" She shrieks, her legs tensing around me.

I grab her hips before she can try to pull away, her

pussy spasming around me like she's trying to push me out. "Shh," I hush her, my mouth against hers. "Focus on my mouth, Taliana. Focus on kissing me."

I don't give her a chance to fight me or voice a protest. Instead, I silence her with my tongue, forcing her to adhere to my command, to let me take care of her the way I know how to.

She responds by digging her nails into me even more, the scent of blood taunting the air.

Little hellion, I think, pleased.

And I finally give in to the instinct to pump my hips forward.

She screams against me, her insides clamping down so hard around me that I nearly come prematurely. Because *fuck*, she's tight. And wet. And hot. And so Godsdamn perfect that, for a minute, I lose all control of my senses.

Then I taste her tears in our kiss and realize she's crying from the pain.

I hush her with a purr, my dragon telling his intended mate that he's proud of her for accepting us inside her, and I draw little patterns against her hip bone in an unspoken vow to give her more.

"You're doing so well," I promise her. "I know it's a lot, little diamond. But your pussy feels so good around me. Soon, you'll see how amazing we are together, how perfectly we *fit*."

She trembles, her fingers releasing me as she spasms beneath me.

I kiss away her tears while I wait for her to acclimate to my size, and continue whispering praise against her mouth. "I'm so grateful for you," I tell her. "You're a fantasy I never knew I needed until now."

Because Gods, I've never been this hard in my life. This pent up. This fucking aroused.

She just feels so damn good. So flaming flawless.

I need to move.

To fuck.

To *rut*.

But I don't want to hurt her. I don't want to *rush* this.

Only, my hips have a mind of their own, my beast raging within me. And I can't stop myself from shifting back and forth inside her. Not harshly. Just a little movement to pacify my urges as I try to regain my control.

"Fuck, Taliana," I breathe, my mouth falling to her neck. "I'm losing my mind here. You just feel so damn incredible."

Her fingers flex on my shoulders, her nails finally leaving my skin. "It hurts."

"I know, sweet diamond. I know." I kiss her throat. "I'm sorry."

"But I…" She clenches around me, making me curse. "I trust you to make me feel good."

I shudder against her. Those words are the encouragement I need to move. To teach her. To *show* her just how good I can make her feel.

She winces as I pull out of her, then jumps when I slam back into her.

I don't give her a chance to think too much about it before I do it again.

And again.

And again.

By the sixth or seventh pump, she's moaning.

Then suddenly she's clawing at me for very different reasons than before, and her svelte hips are driving upward to meet mine. It's like a switch flipped and her wolf took over, allowing us to become feral beasts together as our mouths connect in time with our bodies below.

Her tongue is fierce.

But mine is fiercer.

My docile, obedient Omega is fighting me, her inhibitions seeming to come undone.

And we lose ourselves to our passion. To our animals. To our instincts.

She scratches at my back, and I pound into her pussy like a man possessed. Each punch of my hips draws beautiful cries from her lips, which I promptly swallow with my tongue.

Her wolf growls, the sounds vibrating my chest.

My dragon returns the sound.

Our hands roam. Our mouths duel. And her pussy fucking clamps down around me like she's trying to force me to claim her in the way only an Alpha can.

Normally, I don't allow topping from the bottom. But for this female, I give in. I fucking let her have it, my knot shooting out of my shaft and connecting inside her in a way that has her screaming beneath me.

Only this time, they're screams of pleasure.

Pleasure I echo with a groan as my seed possesses her from the inside out.

It's so fucking intense that I lose my sight.

Then my purr automatically ignites, the sound for my Omega as I nuzzle her neck.

And bite down.

Hard.

Claiming my mate.

My Omega.

My fucking goddess.

Taliana gasps, her eyes widening in shock. And then she's coming again, her sweet cunt pulsing around me as I continue to empty my seed inside her.

It'll be a miracle if my knot ever subsides. I'm so damn

deep in her that I'm pretty sure it'll take hours for me to release her.

Which means she's just going to keep coming and coming.

Probably until she passes out.

Then she'll wake up orgasming again.

"You look so good like this," I tell her on a pant. "Blissed out and so beautifully fucked. Gods, your heat is going to be divine. I'm going to keep you on my cock the entire time, force you to sleep with my knot inside you."

I nuzzle her throat.

"I'm going to take all your holes, too," I whisper. "Teach you how to take me. Learn how to please you. Fuck you into oblivion over and over again. Pierce you. Bite you. Make you mine in every way known to a Drakonian."

She arches into me, still riding the waves of pleasure as she gives me a delirious look. One that tells me she's seconds away from losing consciousness.

And all I can do is smile.

"You're going to wake up screaming," I say. "Then I'm going to kiss you while you continue to come all over my knot, marking me with your precious slick."

Her eyes widen.

Then roll into the back of her head.

I gently kiss her throat, waiting calmly for her to wake.

Which she does on a shriek that ends in my name.

I purr for her. Growl, too. Kiss her. Worship her. Work her through each of her climaxes. And hold her as she continues to fall apart.

By the time my knot subsides, she's incoherent and so alluringly fucked that I immediately want to do it again.

Alas, she's not ready.

I wondered if her heat would be triggered by this, but I can tell by the exhaustion in her features that she hasn't lost her senses to her estrus yet.

Soon, though.

And when it happens, I'm going to adorn her with gold, then make her my queen.

CHAPTER TWENTY-THREE

TALIANA

Everything hurts.

Yet I've never felt more alive.

More *pleased*.

The strawberry Oros places at my lips pleases me even more, as does the warm water around us.

He poured me a bath.

I officially know what utopia feels like.

He presses a kiss to the mark he left on my neck, his chest vibrating at my back. Then he feeds me another berry as he asks, "Feeling any better, printesa mea?"

His knot throbs beneath me, making me wonder if that's the reason he's asking. "Are you wanting to do that again?"

He chuckles. "Yes, very much so. But not tonight. I want to ensure you're recovered before I knot you again."

I shiver at the thought of his knot inside me, how amazing it felt to just let go and allow him to take full control. "It felt... really good."

"Mmm," he hums, kissing his bite mark again. "I would say it felt incredible."

"That, too," I agree, relaxing against him and enjoying another strawberry. He's already washed my hair and skin, having taken us to the shower before drawing this bath.

At first, I didn't understand the purpose.

But now I do.

Because this is divine.

I close my eyes and just let him hold me. Feed me. Purr for me. Caress me. Kiss me. *Claim me.*

Drakonian bonds are unique in that the Omega has to accept the Alpha, too. I know some wolf breeds require it as well.

The claims also need to be done while an Omega is in heat. So although he's technically marked me, it won't be official until my estrus. And it won't be permanent until I accept him back.

What he did was announce his claim. Even though my body is immortal, the crescent scar will remain as a symbol on my skin. He'll either deepen that symbol when I go into heat, or he'll create a matching one somewhere else on my body.

I kind of like the idea of a second bite, one somewhere else, so I can always wear them.

But I want to mark him, too.

Declare my intent.

I just haven't figured out where to bite him.

Sitting up, I spin in the water and straddle him, intent on finding a place. Because I don't want to wait. I want him to be mine just like I'm his.

"Taliana?" he asks, his eyebrow arching upward. "Are you done with the strawberries?"

"No," I tell him, my eyes searching his upper torso. He's like a sculpted masterpiece, all muscular lines and hardness. *Will my teeth even be sharp enough to cut him?* I wonder.

Then I grunt.

Because I'm a wolf.

Of course my teeth will be sharp enough.

"What are you—"

"Shh," I hush him. "I need to focus."

Because this is important.

I need to ensure my claim is seen. He's a desired Alpha. And after that knotting experience, I'm certain other Omegas would be willing to fight for his attention.

But I'm not sharing.

He's mine.

Mine.

Mine.

Mine.

Now, where shall I declare that claim?

My wolf paces inside me, curious and eager. She knows what I'm doing, how important this decision is. We want something everyone will see. And we want it to please our Alpha, too.

He chose my neck.

But I want somewhere that's all mine.

He never wears shirts, I think, eyeing his muscular chest. *Hmm.* My lips curl. *Yes.* I press my hand to his heart, feel the steady rhythm beneath my palm, and lean forward to brush a kiss just over his left pectoral. Then I move down to where my touch rests against him.

My wolf's excitement nearly makes me yip out loud, her eagerness to taste our mate driving me to sink my teeth into his skin before I can even process the movement.

He purrs in response, his hand going to my head to hold me against him as I deepen my claim. His blood touches my tongue, making me moan.

Everything feels light. Perfect. *Warm.*

My soul is satisfied.

My animal calms.

And I feel alive. Complete. *Content.*

I release him and lick my lips, his essence an aphrodisiac that makes me want to do so much more. Yet my body is too replete to try.

So I simply wrap my arms around him and hug him. *My prince. My Oros. My mate.*

"Thank you," he whispers against my ear. "Thank you for being mine. For trusting me. For forgiving me for not telling you who I am. For giving our future a chance. For letting me worship you. For being the perfect mate."

I melt into him. "You haven't even met my wolf yet, so you don't know if I'm perfect or not."

"I don't need to see her to know she's perfect," he tells me, his palm finding my cheek as he eases me back to meet his gaze. "Your wolf is more than accepted by my dragon, Taliana. He sees her worth, and I'll spend eternity ensuring you know how accepted you are here."

He kisses me, his mouth reverent against mine.

"The entire sector knows we're courting," he adds against my lips. "And not a single shifter has commented negatively. You'll soon see that they find you just as worthy as I do, and they will embrace you as their Princess of Gold Sector."

I shiver. Never in a million years could I have dreamt of such a title being bestowed upon me. "I feel like I'm dreaming," I admit aloud. "Like this is all just some glorified fantasy that I've created to cope with my reality."

He chuckles. "No, little diamond. It's just a fairy tale come true."

My brow furrows. "Like the one you told me? Where she cheats and guesses his name?"

His laugh grows and he shakes his head. "Not quite. There are some fairy tales with happy endings."

"Oh? Give me an example."

"Our story," he murmurs. "That's a good example, don't you think?"

"But our story has just begun," I argue. "This is a happy beginning, not a happy ending."

"Hmm, that's fair," he agrees. "Then perhaps we'll just have to create our own fairy tale, one with lots of gold and endless nights of passion."

"Is that your idea of a happily-ever-after?" I ask him, curious.

"My ideal happily-ever-after is anything that involves you, printesa mea," he says, a hint of humor in his voice.

"Why does that sound like there's hidden meaning in your words?" I ask slowly, catching on to the subtlety underlining his words.

"Because you're a fast learner," he murmurs, kissing me on the nose. "But if you like, I can indulge you in a tale. A pleasant one."

I consider the offer and him, then slowly shake my head. "No. I'm content with simply continuing our story."

Amusement flirts with his lips. "I like that idea, printesa mea."

"Good." I place my lips against his. "Then let's write a new chapter in the nest."

"You're not too sore?" he asks.

I shrug. "I suspect there are other things you can teach me."

His grin grows. "Oh, little diamond, you have no idea…"

"I think I have some idea," I say as I rock against his hips. "But let's go see how fast I catch on."

He kisses me long and hard, then pulls back, his golden gaze swirling with intent. "As you wish, Omega."

"As you command, Alpha," I return.

He growls, approval radiating from his expression. "You really are the perfect mate."

My heart skips a beat, my wolf preening inside.

Because for the first time in my life, I wonder if he might be right. If perhaps I really am worthy. And if maybe... this really is... *a fairy tale*.

CHAPTER TWENTY-FOUR
OROS

"I ASSUME YOU'RE HERE TO TALK ABOUT RIO," I SAY AS MY brother ashes into my office. I snuck down here around dawn, leaving Taliana all snuggled up in our nest. The little note I left beside a gold rose will tell her how to find me.

Of course, I suspect her nose will lead her right to me regardless of the letter.

Still, I wanted to be absolutely sure that she could find me.

And I didn't want to wander too far, just in case she needed me.

My dragon was disappointed, his need to fly riding us both. But I placated him with the thought of taking our Omega for a flight once she wakes.

"Keegan's a Stealth Royal," my brother says, drawing me back to his presence in my office.

I arch a brow. "You usually save your sarcasm for after the noon hour."

He grunts and collapses into his favorite chair, his silver eyes grabbing and holding mine. "I wish I were being sarcastic. The bastard woke me up this morning with a blade against my throat."

My eyes widen. "He *what?* Is he still alive?"

"Only because he fucking vanished before I could stab him," Onyx mutters, clearly irritated. "He was making a point."

"That he has a death wish?" I seethe.

"That he could kill us while we slept if he wanted to," my brother says. "He's fucking dangerous."

"No shit." *Flames.* "I'm going to have to kill him." And that's going to seriously upset my intended mate.

"Or we could ally ourselves with him," Onyx offers, surprising me.

"Did he drug you?"

Onyx huffs a laugh. "I'm not completely incapable of making diplomatic choices, brother."

My eyebrow lifts again. "Oh?"

He gives me a look, one that says he's not amused by my disbelief. But rather than chastise me, he just sighs. "We need to let Rio bring his sister here, Oros."

I gape at him. Not only did he dismiss the opportunity to try to rib me back, but he also just uttered words I never thought I would hear from him.

So I do what I need to do and take his advice seriously. "Tell me why," I say to him. Not because I'm questioning his opinion, but because I want to understand how he arrived at that decision.

Onyx drums his fingers along the leather arm of the chair, his silver gaze taking on an earnest gleam as he stares at me. "I don't like Rio. I never have and likely never will. But the archaic blood vows of the past deserve to burn. And from what Rio has said, his father disagrees. He wants Rio to send his sister to Wes."

My jaw ticks, my gaze narrowing slightly. Our father

would have said the same—to follow through with the blood vow. If Onyx and I hadn't rid ourselves of his influence at a young age, we might feel similarly.

But our Omega mother raised us.

And arranged matings are not our preference as a result.

"It would be the easier route," my brother goes on. "Rio acknowledged that. However, he refuses to sacrifice his sister to a potential monster, and he has no desire to entertain an alliance with Obsidian Sector. The recent assault on Lanzarote solidified his opinion on the matter."

"So you believe him when he says he didn't let Basalt through Gibraltar," I infer.

"Yes. Just as I think he might be onto something regarding Wes actually being in charge." Onyx elaborates on why he feels this way, sharing with me all the details Keegan provided after waking him up at knifepoint. "It's compelling information, particularly as he proved he's more than capable of bypassing standard security protocols to spy on others."

My lips twitch at the aggrieved nature of his tone. "I can't believe you let him live."

He grunts. "He didn't give me much of a choice."

"So he bested you?" I ask, surprised.

"Did you miss the part where I told you he vanished into thin air?"

"We can do that, too," I point out.

"Yeah, except his knife didn't disappear, and neither did his voice," my brother replies flatly. "He was standing right fucking there, but all my blade met was air. It was like something out of a childhood nightmare."

"Hmm." I'm not sure I like this development. "Is he going to be a problem?"

"Only if you hurt his daughter." Onyx's gaze flashes

with knowledge as he takes in the crescent mark on my chest. "I assume you've made your intentions clear, too?"

"I have."

He nods. "Then no, he won't be a problem. Which brings me back to my ally comment—I think we need to work with him and Riordan. But if we're going to accept Rio's sister, then we need to make some arrangements for her safety."

"Sounds like you've already started planning," I say slowly.

"Not planning so much as thinking." He frowns. "She's going to need a guardian, and I can't figure out who to assign to her."

"I'm sure we have a few capable Alphas who won't mind guarding her," I say, not understanding his concern.

Onyx palms the back of his neck, his expression uncharacteristically wary. "I don't think this is going to be a normal guardianship."

He goes on to share some of the details he learned from Rio, each one impressing me more than the previous admission. "It sounds like she has a penchant for trouble," I muse.

"Yeah. Oh, and she can ash," he mutters. "Which means she needs an Alpha who can leash her like Rio does."

"That severely limits who can guard her." Only my brother and I possess the ability to control another's ability to ash.

"I know." He gives me a look. "And you're obviously too occupied for the task."

"I also don't want the task."

"And I do?" He sounds utterly miserable.

Yet I can't help pointing out, "You're the one suggesting we take on this burden."

"Because it's the right move." He drops his hand back to the arm of the chair and meets my gaze. "Obsidian Sector is expanding, which means alliances are more important now than ever. Riordan is our strongest option outside of the surrounding wolf clans."

I nod, agreeing with that assessment.

"And if Obsidian Sector has truly allied with the Djinn, it's even more imperative that we solidify our partnership with Riordan."

"How's he planning to handle his father?" I ask, curious as to where Silver Sector—the territory his father leads—will fall in this arrangement. "Does Rio intend to inform Bronze of where the Omega Princess is headed?"

Onyx's pupils flare at my choice of term for the Omega, but she is indeed a princess. Her father, Bronze, and her brother, Rio, are both Alpha Princes. That marks her as royal by blood.

"When I asked about Bronze, Rio said not to worry about the nuance and that he would handle the fallout."

"Hmm," I hum. "So long as he doesn't disclose her location, then fine. But I don't want to battle Bronze for custody of his little princess."

"I'm more worried about his little princess escaping our protection and putting herself in harm's way," my brother mutters. "She's going to be a nightmare."

I smile. "Something tells me I'm going to enjoy watching you try to tame her."

"Maybe Rio's overexaggerating," my brother says, ignoring my jibe. "It seems like something he would do."

I don't reply, mainly because it's clear my brother isn't paying attention to me at all now. He's too busy sussing out the situation with Rio and his sister.

I leave him to his thoughts as I type a message to Rio.

You somehow convinced my brother that we should help you. I'm both impressed and furious. The next time you want to know something about my sector, be Alpha enough to visit on your own to discover the truth. I look forward to punching you in the face when you arrive. We'll talk after.

I'm about to hit Send as my brother says, "I'm going to need at least a week to prepare for her arrival. I want to… fortify a guest suite."

My eyebrow inches upward. "Which guest suite?"

"The one attached to my room," he replies, sounding tired already.

"You mean the second bedroom you use as an office?" I ask. He technically has a space on the opposite end of this floor, but he only uses it when hosting a meeting with one of our generals.

"Yeah." He rubs a hand over his face. "I'll just move everything up here and ask Savan to help me with some furniture for our new ward."

"Oh, please call her that," I murmur.

He rolls his eyes. "You're enjoying this far too much. Maybe I should suggest that you babysit the brat instead?"

"Actually, on second thought, lead with that. I'm sure she'll react beautifully to being called a brat," I drawl.

My brother growls in response. "Just for that, I'm calling you Rumpelstiltskin the next time we address the court."

I lift a shoulder in a partial shrug. "Do your worst, Silverstiltskin."

With that, I add a final line to my missive—*Onyx needs more time to make appropriate arrangements for your stay. Reach out to him to discuss further.*

I carefully leave out the details about Rio bringing his sister, as I don't want that in writing in case anyone intercepts the message. But Rio will understand the context of what I'm telling him.

And if for some reason he doesn't, Onyx will fill him in.

"I'll need to prepare myself for the headache you and Rio are going to induce with all your incessant bickering," I mutter as I hit the Send button. "But at least you two have figured out how to converse without me being present."

Something that's going to be increasingly important as my Omega goes into heat.

Speaking of... I think, my nose twitching as her scent nears. "Anything else?" I ask my brother, suddenly very eager for him to leave.

His brow furrows, then he glances toward the balcony and the stairs that ascend to my room. "When would you like me to take over as temporary Prince of Gold Sector?"

I smile. "Now would be nice." Taliana isn't in heat yet, but I hope to change that today.

Because I have an idea.

One I intend to run by her after I take her for a flight.

"Are there any pertinent items I need to be aware of?" Onyx asks, all business as Taliana appears on the stairs.

"I think you're aware of everything that's coming," I tell him, referring to Rio and his sister. "I trust you to handle the arrangements."

He nods. "I'll be naming Savan as temporary Second."

"That's fine." He's one of our most trustworthy generals. He also likely would have been assigned as Taliana's guardian had I not stepped into the position.

That was why my brother told him to escort her to Doctor Taylor that first day.

And why I dismissed Savan when I saw his reactions to her fear.

She wasn't his to soothe.

She's mine.

A fact that resonates as she enters my office wearing nothing but a sheet.

"Consider the sector handled, brother," Onyx says, his silver eyes flashing with a hint of emotion. Surprisingly, it looks a lot like approval. "Princess," he murmurs to my intended mate as he stands.

Her eyes widen as he inclines his head in a show of respect.

"I'll ensure you both have everything you need," he adds, then straightens. "See you in a week or so."

He vanishes before I can reply, leaving my little diamond blinking. "He didn't have to leave," she whispers.

"Oh, he did." I push away from my desk and slowly prowl toward her. "You're on the verge of your heat, and you're mine. It's dangerous for any Alpha to be near you right now."

Her small nose crinkles. "Because I might induce a rut?"

"Because I might kill anyone who looks at you the wrong way," I correct her. "I'm possessive, printesa mea. I'm the only one allowed to be near you right now." I wrap my palm around her nape, pulling her into me for a long, sensuous kiss.

She's practically panting by the time I release her, causing my lips to curl.

"Let's go for a flight," I murmur, my gaze roaming over her makeshift cloak. "And lose the sheet."

CHAPTER TWENTY-FIVE

TALIANA

"A FLIGHT?" I REPEAT, A FLURRY OF BUTTERFLIES blossoming to life in my belly. "As in…"

"As in my dragon wants to take you for a ride," Oros says, his words a breath against my lips. "Now drop the sheet, and I'll shift for you."

Warmth engulfs my being, my hands trembling as I release the fabric from my shoulders and let it fall to the floor.

His gaze dances down to my breasts, then to the apex between my thighs, and he unfastens his pants.

He's cloakless and shoeless, leaving his trousers as the only item he needs to remove. Yet he does it painfully slowly, like he's purposely prolonging my anticipation.

Or maybe he's ensuring he doesn't hurt himself.

Because he's hard. *Very, very hard*. His knot is a throbbing bulb at the base of his shaft, one I long to lick.

"You look thirsty, little diamond," he murmurs, his hands pushing the black fabric down his thighs. "I'd offer you something to drink, but my beast is demanding that I satisfy his needs first." He kicks off his pants and holds a hand out for me. "Come fly with me, little diamond. I want everyone in the sector to see you on my back."

"I've never been flying before," I admit while placing my palm against his, my heart hammering in my rib cage.

He frowns. "Does the thought frighten you?"

I shake my head. "No, it excites me. I've always wanted to fly."

His irises glitter as he leads me out onto the balcony, the sun reflecting off his beautiful features. "I'm very pleased to be your first, printesa mea," he murmurs, pulling me in for another kiss before pressing his lips to my ear. "And I fully intend to be your last, too."

Before I can process those words, he's already stepping back and shifting.

My lips part as he reveals his dragon form, his golden scales immediately familiar. Because I've seen him like this before.

A week ago.

When meeting with the Royal Court.

"You sniffed me that day," I acknowledge aloud, utterly in awe at the visual unraveling before me. Because he's stunning. Majestic. Absolutely breathtaking.

His beast gives a little purr, like he's pleased by my recognition, or perhaps he can see my appreciation. It has to be obvious. I'm practically gaping at him, and I can feel my lips stretching into a stupid grin.

But he's just so gorgeous.

Something I tell him out loud now and I swear his dragon preens in response. Then he dips his head to the ground and releases a loud, commanding rumble. It's not a growl but a deep purr that has me moving toward him without hesitation.

I can't believe I'm about to fly.

It's like a dream.

A fantasy I never thought would exist.

Yet here I am, seconds away from climbing onto a dragon's back. And not just any dragon, a Drakon Alpha. A prince. *My mate.*

Except, I have no idea how to mount him. "You're so big," I whisper, absolutely in awe of his size. "When we first met, I only saw your claws and golden scales." I nearly reach for him, suddenly longing to touch him.

He leans toward me like he knows, and I give in to the urge, his scales surprisingly soft and sleek. *And shimmering with power.*

I shiver as his energy slides up my arms, creating a thin armor against my skin. It's similar to what he usually wears, only it expands beyond my arms to my chest.

I gasp as the soft metal forms over my nipples, the kiss of magic both sensual and arousing.

The gold spreads to cover my breasts, creating a bra of sorts, one that should be uncomfortable but isn't.

"Why does this feel like silk?" I ask him, studying my arm. "I know it's gold. But it moves with me like it's fabric, not metal."

He doesn't answer me, just purrs like he's pleased that I'm enjoying his enchantment.

Which I very much am. Especially the way it warms and cools against my skin.

The sensation slips lower as a delicate chain forms at the center of my gold bodice, the shiny strand sliding down along my belly toward the apex between my thighs.

I jump when the metal reaches my pelvis, my eyes widening as the strand weaves a delicate pattern against my skin to create a pair of matching bottoms.

"You just made me gold lingerie," I breathe, my clit throbbing as his bespelled armor settles right against my sensitive flesh.

Moons…

I'm not sure I want to fly anymore.

Instead, I want him to take me back to the nest and tease me with more of his power.

Except a saddle is already forming on his back.

Along with stirrups.

And reins.

I run my fingers along the enchanted metal. "This is amazing," I whisper, infatuated with his talent.

His magic seems to hum all around me, his gold claiming me intimately and drawing me closer to him. I'm barely aware of my actions as I slip my bare foot into the stirrup and pull myself up into the harness he created.

Almost instantly, the metal shifts to form straps around my ankles and calves, flat sandals forming on my feet in lieu of the former stirrups.

Only, I seem to be connected to him, the straps coming from his scales to secure my legs on either side.

The seat beneath me changes as well, holding me in place on his back as he stands to his full height.

I yelp, leaning down to grab his neck.

And he rumbles in reply, the sound mysteriously like a chuckle.

Then he jumps straight off the balcony without any warning.

I scream as we spin into a free fall, the air whooshing past us so fast and hard that the sound carries away in our wake.

But just as I start to worry that something has gone horribly wrong, Oros flares out his wings and guides us into a controlled glide through the air.

My eyes widen, my mouth agape.

And a laugh leaves me. A laugh born of excitement. Of amazement. Of pure joy.

Because this… this is *so much* better than I could have ever imagined.

I've seen my father fly, but never dared ask for a ride. It was forbidden in Obsidian Sector; only those with wings were allowed to take to the sky.

All our travel between the sectors and the nomad lands was done by speedboat. Never by soaring through the air.

I lift my arms, flapping them in time with Oros's wings, and pretend I'm a pure-blood dragon, too. Pretend that my beast isn't a wolf but a creature with the freedom to fly.

My animal grumbles at that, clearly miffed that I'm longing for something other than her. But I can't help my deep-seated need to embrace my inner Drakonian. It's part of who I am. Who I wish I could be.

Except…

Is that true? I wonder, my gaze taking in my surroundings as I embrace the experience of flight. It feels so good to be up here, to feel the wind on my face.

Yet I've felt this before, too.

While running on four paws.

Oh, but the view is different. Everything is smaller from up here. Like I'm existing above the world rather than in it.

Which gives me a slight pang.

Because I… I *like* being in the thick of things.

This is all still magnificent and more than I ever dreamt it to be, but the similarities are unexpected.

The sun on my back.

The air currents swirling around me.

The sensation of freedom.

But what's even more unexpected than the similarities is the realization that I miss the earth.

I miss sensing the trees against my fur. The dirt beneath my paws. The scent of nature tickling my snout.

I miss being a wolf.

How utterly surprising.

What I enjoy most right now is being with Oros. Having his gold all around me. His beast between my legs. The sensation of being protected and safe while soaring through the clouds. Knowing he cares for me. And understanding that he's mine.

The flight itself is almost irrelevant. It's all about my connection to him and how his power makes me feel.

No, more than that. His *dominance*. His Alpha prowess. His all-encompassing passion.

I shiver, an exotic twist of emotions seeming to swirl through me all at once.

Excitement.

Contentment.

Adoration.

Warmth.

A sense of freedom followed by the need to run.

It's confusing and overwhelming, yet calming at the same time.

I… I feel so much.

And those feelings only intensify as Oros takes us downward toward the sea.

I giggle as he skims the surface, causing a mist to form around us.

I gasp as he shoots back up again.

Then gape at the view of a glorious beach ahead.

We've left the main island. This is somewhere several miles away, the land mostly black like it's all composed of ash.

He doesn't take us down to land, just circles the peak before flying us over the sea again.

After a second island, I realize he's giving me another tour, this time of the other isles under his control.

They seem to be scantly populated with just a few dragons lounging about in the sun. When I see a pack of wolves, he flies lower to let me wave.

They howl in response, the sound one that fills my heart with glee. Because I recognize that welcoming call.

They accept me here.

I'm home.

Well and truly… home.

That sensation of acceptance grows as some dragons join us in the air, their majestic wings varying in color and size. A few do dips and twirls like they're showing off for our benefit. Others simply coast along in silent camaraderie.

Until we're left alone once more.

That's when Oros truly begins to descend toward a small island in the distance, the shoreline dotted with overgrown trees. It appears to be deserted, making me wonder why he's chosen this particular beach as we land.

The water is beautiful, though. The deep blue color is a startling contrast to the black sand beneath.

Oros lowers his head, his golden enchantment unweaving to allow me to move.

At first I don't, my legs having fallen asleep during our flight. I'd been too caught up in my emotions and thoughts to even realize it, but I feel the tingles now as I try to move my lower limbs.

Oros doesn't speed me along, just waits while I gather my bearings, and purrs.

The rumble grows softer when I finally descend, then disappears entirely as he returns to his human form.

Eyes the color of glittering gold stare down at me, his lips curling into a satisfied smile. "I've never flown like that before."

I frown. "To here?"

"No, I come here all the time. I meant with a passenger on my back." He grabs my nape to tug me in for a kiss. "It was the best kind of foreplay, feeling you encased in my gold while riding my dragon through the sky."

His words elicit a shiver from deep within, one that intensifies as his metal whispers across my skin. Glancing down, I see that it's dissolving into mystical dust, leaving me as naked as him.

Something he's definitely enjoying, his heated gaze tells me. As does the impressive knot pulsing against my lower belly.

I swallow, my arousal piquing once more. But before I can voice it or demand that he kiss me again, Oros says, "Shift."

I blink at him. "Wh-what?"

"Shift," he repeats. "You've properly met my dragon. So now I want to meet your wolf."

My lashes flutter again, my heart skipping several beats. "I… It'll cause…" I trail off, clearing my throat. "I'll probably go into heat." That's what Doctor Taylor said, anyway. She might be wrong.

But that's not actually the reason for my hesitation.

Something I think Oros may know because he arches a brow and asks, "Is that a problem? Are you not ready for your estrus?"

"I…" I can't lie to him. It would be wrong. "I'm nervous, but I'm not afraid of it like I used to be. And I know you'll take care of me during my heat."

"Oh, I'll more than take care of you, printesa mea," he murmurs, his gaze glimmering with seductive promises as he brushes his lips against mine. "I'm going to pleasure you in ways you've never even dreamed of. But first, I want to see your wolf."

A fluttering sensation stirs in my stomach, one born of nerves this time more than excitement.

No one has ever asked to meet my wolf before. Everyone prefers I keep her hidden.

It goes against all my instincts to show her off, especially to a Drakonian Alpha. "Are you sure?" I ask, unable to hold the quivering note back from my voice.

"Absolutely," he says, all confidence. "I want to see every part of you, printesa me. And that includes meeting your beautiful wolf."

Beautiful is certainly not an adjective I've heard in reference to my beast before. Most Alphas just call her an abomination. Others say she's a mutt or a lesser being.

Then there are those who looked upon her with open disgust, spitting in her direction and telling me never to shift in their presence again. They called my creature *dirty*.

My heart will shatter into a thousand pieces if Oros does that.

I… I may never recover.

What if—

"Taliana," he says, his palm resembling a brand against my nape. "Please show me your wolf."

It's not a command. Just a soft request.

One that makes me shiver again.

Because I don't want to deny my intended mate.

I just hope he doesn't—

"She needs to know that I adore her, too," Oros tells me. "And there's only one way to prove it to her."

My brow furrows. "You adore my wolf?"

"I adore *you*," he tells me. "All of you. Every part of you." He kisses my cheek, then presses his lips to my ear. "*Especially* your wolf."

My animal practically dances inside me like she understood that.

Or maybe she just feels my resolve melting.

Her excitement causes my heart to race, the overabundance of energy making me realize just how badly she wants me to let her out. I always keep her locked away, mostly for our survival.

But here... here she doesn't have to hide. *I* don't have to hide.

I'm not an abomination. Or a mutt. Or a dirty shifter.

I'm a hybrid. An Omega of mixed origin.

And this male wants me to be his mate.

I need to let him prove to me what that means. I need to see his acceptance. His open appraisal. His *approval.*

Why am I hiding? I wonder, taking a step back from him. *Why am I denying my Alpha what he wants?*

No.

That isn't even the question I should be asking.

Why am I denying my wolf? is the better query.

I don't want to deny her anymore. Suppress her. Ignore her. Keep her caged away.

I... I want to let her fly in her own way. To pound across the earth. To be *unleashed.*

So I do something I've never been allowed to do before. Something I didn't even realize I needed or wanted.

I take a few more steps back, my toes skimming the edge of the ocean.

Then I close my eyes.

And finally let my wolf... *free.*

CHAPTER TWENTY-SIX
TALIANA

Heat overwhelms every inch of my being as my wolf breathes for the first time in what feels like years. My father always supervised my shifts in the past, his presence required as a guard.

But now I have Oros.

Only, he isn't hovering over me in a protective manner the way my father usually would. Instead, he's staring at me with a look of astonishment, like he can't believe I exist.

I shrink back inside, terrified of what he's about to say.

I warned him.

I told him I'm a wolf.

So he can't be that surprised by my appearance.

But maybe... maybe he thought—

"You're even more beautiful than I imagined," he whispers, causing me to freeze inside. "*Flames*, printesa mea." He falls to his knees before me, his gaze holding mine. "I knew you would be majestic, but this..." He reaches out a hand, causing my wolf to instantly lean into him, eager for his touch. "Wow. You're *exquisite*."

My animal gives her version of a purr, dazzled by his praise. She might not understand his words, but she understands admiration. And she is *very* pleased.

Her eyes close, stealing my vision.

But I don't care.

Because I can feel Oros's touch as he explores my animal's coat.

I can sense the truth in his words.

And for the first time in my life, I feel worthy. Not only that, but cherished and respected and *wanted*.

"Will you run for me?" Oros asks, causing my beast to look at him once more. "I flew for you. Now it's your turn to—"

My animal takes off before he can even finish, too eager to let herself fly.

His words were so contrary to the ones my father would whisper.

Be careful, Tali.

Don't go too fast; I have to be able to keep up with you on two legs.

My dragon can't stay that low to the ground in the forest.

My father meant well. I know that. But hearing him in my head now almost makes me slow.

However, a burst of golden light to my right has my wolf running faster instead. Because Oros is following us in dragon form, his speed matching ours as his wings beat through the sky.

My animal's tongue lolls to the side, then she darts to the left, leaving the beach and heading straight for the trees ahead. They're not thick here, or even that tall, allowing Oros to fly right along overhead as my wolf's paws race across the earth.

It's exhilarating.

Amazing.

Freeing.

My father would be growling right now, demanding that I stop.

But not Oros.

He's above me, keeping pace with ease and coaxing us onward with his loud purr. I'm not even sure how I hear him; he has to be a good fifty feet up in the sky. Yet I feel his rumble like it's right next to my ear, the vibration teasing every inch of my being.

I tremble, my insides pulsing to life with renewed warmth.

My estrus, I realize.

But my wolf isn't ready to stop.

She's running faster than she's ever run in her life, darting between trees, exploring this island like she was destined to be here.

Home, she seems to be thinking. *This is home.*

And I couldn't agree more.

She jumps into a clearing ahead, finding a lagoon of sorts. I can see the vast ocean in the distance, but this area seems to be framed by white rocks rather than black sand.

It's shallow, too, granting me a clear view of the bottom.

My wolf eyes it with interest, then frolics into the sea, the water providing instant relief to the burn stealing over my fur.

Or rather, my *skin* beneath the fur.

Oros swoops down to join us, his wings causing the water to spray upward in a gentle wave that has my wolf yipping in delight.

She doesn't shy away or sputter or express a single ounce of displeasure.

No. She simply *pounces* instead.

His dragon falls to his back, his wings pillowing his fall as my wolf lands on his exposed belly.

Suddenly, we're rolling through the lagoon.

What a ridiculous sight we must make, I think, laughing inside at the sheer inaneness of this situation—his much larger form wrestling with my petite animal.

Yet somehow… it works.

And I've never been more elated in my life.

We're playing, I realize. *My wolf is playing with a dragon.*

I can barely believe it.

But it becomes all the more real when he pins me beneath his massive body and places his mouth at my neck.

My wolf instantly submits, more than happy to be beneath him.

He growls low in his throat, the demand clear to both me and my animal. He wants us to shift. Though, he doesn't truly command it. Otherwise, I would already be turning back into a human. Because powerful Alphas can absolutely force transformations on others, and many do.

However, Oros doesn't. He simply releases my throat and stares down at me expectantly.

The moment I transition, I'm going to go into heat. I can feel it in my belly, the warmth swirling in wait.

This will hurt, I acknowledge. *But Oros will make me feel good.*

I hope he can see that truth in my gaze as I stare up at him through my wolf's eyes. Because I might not be able to voice it when I finish shifting.

His golden orbs watch me steadily as my fur recedes, his dragon the epitome of possessiveness and protectiveness in his position over me.

By the time I finish, I'm already panting. "So hot," I manage to tell him, a convulsive shudder overtaking me. "*Oros.*"

I need him.

And I need him *now*.

My stomach clenches as lava pours through my veins. My vision goes temporarily dark, the sensations too overwhelming for me to process.

All I am is heat.

A puddle of desire.

Weeping from the profound urge to touch myself between my thighs.

But when my hands move in that direction, I find them suddenly locked in a grip over my head.

My eyelids flutter, catching on a flash of gold. *Intent. Dominant. Alpha.*

I spread my thighs, inviting him in, begging for his touch, his *knot*.

"Stay with me, printesa mea," a deep voice demands.

I don't know what he means. I'm obviously here. Where does he intend for me to go?

"*Taliana*," he tries again, his tone making me gasp as it curls around me in a fist of dominance that I can't ignore.

"Oros," I breathe, both shocked by his commanding hold over me and confused by what just happened.

"Good girl," he murmurs, his lips claiming mine.

I have no idea what he's praising me for, but I accept the reward he offers with his tongue. Because ohhh, how I love kissing this male. This Alpha. *My intended mate.*

His cock is hot against my core, making me long to feel him inside me. But something else enters me instead. *His fingers*, I realize in the next beat. He has one hand between my legs and the other holding my wrists over my head.

I arch into him, needing more. Demanding friction. Requiring *connection*.

My nipples are so hard that I practically scream when

they meet his muscular chest. Everything is so sensitive. I…
I can barely think. I can only *feel*.

"Stay with me," he says against my mouth. "I need you
to remember this."

I don't know what he means.

But I try to obey him anyway.

His tongue captivates mine as his fingers fuck me
below. I'm so close yet so far away. His touch isn't enough.
It's… it's a tease.

I sink my teeth into his lower lip, telling him without
words that I need more.

He growls in response.

Then purrs when I wrap my legs around his hips.

"Please," I beg, pushing up into his palm. "*Please.*"

"Shh," he hushes me, adding another finger below. "I
don't want to hurt you."

My wolf snarls inside me, irritated by his holding back.
She fought his dragon, played with him, *wrestled*. We are
not weak. We are *ready*.

Oros hums, his grip tightening on my wrists. "You're
trying to challenge me, hmm?"

"*Knot me.*"

He nuzzles my nose, his mouth tauntingly close to
mine. "And now you're issuing commands." His lips
whisper across my cheek to my ear. "As my future mate, I'll
allow it." He lowers his touch to my throat, his teeth
sinking in without warning.

And then I feel him at my entrance, his hardness a
threat to my sanity, to my very sense of being.

I forgot how big he is, how intense it is to—

He thrusts inside, drawing a scream unlike any I've
ever released.

But it quickly turns into a moan at the sensation of
being full.

Oh, it hurts. It hurts *a lot*. Only, it's a good hurt. It's the right hurt. It's the hurt I crave.

Because I'm wet. I'm ready. And I *need* more.

Which I tell him with a growl, one driven out of me by my wolf. Just as she urges me to sink my teeth into his shoulder.

Which I do.

Harshly.

Drawing blood.

Claiming my mate.

He snarls in response, biting me again on the neck.

Then suddenly my hands are free as he grips my hips and slams into me without mercy. I try to meet his thrusts, but I'm a slave to his motions, his palms placing me right where he wants me for each harsh thrust.

It's animalistic. Primal. *Divine insanity.*

I'm not sure when he releases my throat or how I let go of his shoulder, but in a span of seconds, we're kissing each other with a ferocity that rivals our movements below.

My heart pounds in my chest, my thighs clenching around his. Every part of me is alive. Ready. *Demanding his knot.*

I squeeze around him, my insides bereft and aching.

Complete me, I try to tell him. *Make me yours.*

One of his palms leaves my hips to wrap around my throat, his dominant hold exactly what I crave as he devours me with his mouth. Owns me with his cock. Commands me with his presence.

My Alpha, a part of me sighs even as I scream his name aloud.

Because I'm so close, walking right along the precipice of that beautiful sensation, the one he awoke within me.

I chase the heat, embrace the pleasure-pain, and jump headfirst into the oblivion waiting for me below.

Only, it's not enough.

Gods, it's nowhere near enough.

Tears trickle down my cheeks, words of need leave my lips, but every begging statement is swallowed by my Alpha. My mate.

He's driving me mad.

Holding me on the brink, forcing me to walk this tenuous line between misery and rapture.

I weep. I scream. I scratch his back. I *bite.*

And still he fucks me, holding me with his hands, squeezing my throat as he tells me to "Hold on."

I don't want to *hold on.* I want to—

Stars explode around me as the most fulfilling sensation spasms throughout my lower abdomen. *His knot. Inside me. Throbbing. Pulsing. Ohhh… oh, yes…*

My nails dig into his shoulders, some part of my mind finally understanding what he meant when he told me to hold on.

But I no longer care.

Not with this euphoric explosion swallowing me whole.

Yes, yes…

I'm lost.

Free.

Floating in ecstasy.

Knotted by my Alpha.

Mated.

I feel him inside me, not just with his knot, but his mind connecting to mine. A whisper of emotion followed by an avalanche of thought.

You're mine now, printesa mea, he murmurs into my mind. *Mine to love. Mine to knot. Mine to create a life with.*

My lashes lift a little at that last part, the final vestiges of my sanity flickering in and out. *Create a life… a whelp?*

We agreed to wait, didn't we?

Or is that what I want?

I can no longer say.

Because all I desire is him. His touch. His tongue. His hands. *His seed.*

And I tell him that by wrapping myself around him.

"More," I demand.

I think he chuckles in response. *My knot is still inside you, little diamond. But as soon as it recedes, I'll fuck you again. Then I'm piercing your tits with my gold.*

A shiver works through me. I like the idea of him marking me. Claiming me. Making me his in all ways. *Yes.*

His lips brush across mine, and something soft touches my back.

Our nest, I recognize.

Yes, Omega, my Alpha replies with a mental kiss. *Welcome home, Princess.*

CHAPTER TWENTY-SEVEN
OROS

I STARE AT THE GOLD RINGS EMBEDDED IN TALIANA'S nipples, pleased by her markings. She barely stirred when I pierced her hours ago, the enchanted metal holding a magical property that numbed the pain while also ensuring her immortal form didn't try to continuously heal the tiny holes.

"So pretty," I muse, leaning down to kiss each charm.

There's a third piercing in her belly button, that one holding a bar with a rare gold diamond charm on the end.

"It's perfect," I tell her sleeping form. "So perfect that I think I'll wake you with my knot."

She's exhausted but still very much in heat.

It's been three days of constant fucking, which I've very much enjoyed. The hardest part is ensuring she eats between sessions.

Oh, her immortal form can withstand days of sex without sustenance. But I like her energized. And it's fun to find creative ways to convince her to accept food.

Flavoring it with my seed seems to be a popular motivator.

I rather like how much of me she's swallowed, both from coming down her throat and by feeding her my fingers after dipping them into her dripping heat.

She's so beautiful like this, all sexed up and mine.

The only way it could be better would be if a part of me was growing inside her.

Alas, I took the proper pill to ensure that doesn't happen yet.

I press my palm to her belly.

"Maybe you'll want a babe by your next heat," I say, my thumb teasing the diamond resting just inside her belly button.

"But I'll wait until you tell me you're ready," I go on, aware that she not only can't hear me right now, but wouldn't understand me even if she were awake and listening.

"Although, fair warning," I whisper, my mouth traveling back up to her breasts to kiss the crescent claiming mark there. "Once you give me permission to breed you, I'll never stop."

Because I want her full of our babes. A whole brood of dragon whelps and wolf pups.

I admit all that out loud as I slide my dick inside her slick channel and start to slowly fuck her, my mind thinking of our future and how amazing she'll look rounded with our child.

Flames, I've never been so obsessed with the idea in my existence.

But now I can't stop thinking about it.

Maybe it's the contraceptive.

Or maybe it's just this female.

I'm addicted to her. In fucking love with her. Which is crazy and fast, but I just don't care. She was made for me and I was made for her.

We fit.

Fuck, do we fit… Her pussy clamps down around me as though agreeing with my thought. Even asleep, she still takes me perfectly.

"Fires, you're exquisite, printesa mea," I tell her with a groan, my knot throbbing with the demand to be released.

I worked myself up by admiring my handiwork, her piercings everything I desired them to be.

"I want to add more," I admit, thinking about other places to claim her. "Maybe your clit."

Or perhaps that's too much.

But I need everyone to know this female is mine.

"Hmm, or I'll just make you wear more gold panties," I say, thinking of her outfit from the other day when she rode my dragon. "Yes. More of those. Every day. All day. Always in gold. *My* gold."

Her cunt pulses in response, though I suspect that's more from my movements inside her than my words.

Still, I choose to accept that squeeze as an agreement and take her harder in response. Thanking her with my cock for being mine. Driving her to the brink of pleasure. Forcing her to join me in oblivion.

She moans, still asleep but clearly aware of my presence inside her.

"Don't open your eyes yet," I say, savagely fucking her now. "I don't want you to wake until you're thrashing on my cock."

Another clench.

Another deep moan.

She's so close.

But she won't tumble over the edge until my knot is deep inside her.

I palm her breast, teasing her nipple, then lean down to

sink my teeth into her neck in the same place I claimed her days ago.

More slick spills from her tight sheath, warming my flesh as I pound into her. I'm not holding back, aware that in this state, she can take anything and everything I give her.

"So fucking perfect," I growl, loving the way her body accepts my brutality and takes every inch of my cock. "So. Fucking. *Mine*."

My knot shoots into her, claiming her in the way only an Alpha can, and causes her eyelids to fly open as she screams out her pleasure for me.

"Beautiful," I purr, loving that she's crying from the onslaught of sensation. I know part of it hurts, but the rapture overwhelms the ache, giving her a semblance of rightness.

Her little nails dig into my shoulders, her legs wrapping around me in a not-so-subtle demand for more.

However, I can't move yet. Not until my knot subsides.

So I reach between us to rub her clit instead.

She mewls as hot waves of ecstasy wash over her, driving her into a downward spiral of intense oblivion.

Her pretty starburst eyes look up at me in devotion, my Omega utterly lost to her Alpha's touch. To *my* touch.

She trusts me.

And that gift is one I will never take for granted.

I tell her that with my mouth, kissing her gently before licking away her tears. "You're amazing, Princess Taliana," I tell her. "Amazing and mine. And I'm going to take care of you for eternity."

She flexes her hips against me, as if to say I can start fulfilling that vow right now by continuing to fuck her.

I chuckle and ease her back down with my purr. "As soon as my knot is ready, I'll take you again." I press my thumb into her clit before she can complain. "Just ride out the orgasm with me, Omega. Take my seed. And if you're a good girl, I'll let you lick me clean."

She shivers, her pupils dilating in response.

My mate likes that idea.

As do I.

Which is why I guide her downward several minutes later and lie back as she pleasures me with her mouth.

"You're getting so good at that," I tell her, pleased with how eager she's been to learn.

She sucks hard in response, then draws her teeth along my shaft while her hand squeezes my knot.

"Mmm," I hum, momentarily lost to her ministrations. "Keep doing that, Omega. Don't stop until I tell you to."

She obeys, her tongue tracing my dick up to the tip before her mouth swallows me whole again.

"Such a skilled Omega," I praise her. "I think you've earned a reward."

Her eyes, drunk on lust, lazily meet mine while my cock remains in her mouth.

"Come up here," I demand. "Put me inside you and ride me."

She releases me with a pop, her expression hungry. But her tits grab my attention as she starts to crawl, the gold tips swaying with her movements.

"I'm so fucking in love with this view," I say, pulling her the rest of the way up and settling her in my lap.

My head finds her entrance without hesitation, sliding right inside her as she seats herself completely. Then I sit up and kiss her. *Hard.*

And force her to move, to take her pleasure, to demand my knot once more.

It takes longer this time, my body in need of a slight reprieve.

But Taliana is fierce. A queen. A fucking Goddess riding my cock.

And my body is a slave to her needs.

"*Fuck*, Taliana," I groan, my knot shooting out of me once more to connect us on a plane of dark intensity, one that nearly knocks her out again.

Only, I manage to keep her with me by kissing her gently. By caressing her with my hands. By loving her with my tongue.

I lick away more tears.

Chase away some of her whimpers.

And purr for her the way a mate should.

She sighs, satisfied and replete, at least for the moment.

"You're my everything now," I confide softly. "My beautiful wolf. My strong Omega. *My ideal mate.*" I press my lips to hers, hoping she understands what I'm saying, but knowing she probably doesn't.

So I content myself with opening my mind to her and letting her feel my affection.

You are worthy.

You are perfect.

And you, my darling Taliana, are mine.

CHAPTER TWENTY-EIGHT

TALIANA

MMM, BURNING WOOD.

Warmth on a chilled night.

Alpha seed.

Sex.

My wolf stretches languidly inside me, pleased by the scents of our nest. *Our safe haven.*

We're finally safe. Claimed. *Mated.*

That last realization has me peeking out through my lashes, searching for my Alpha.

I find him standing beside the nest with a tray in his hands. I wait, expecting him to join me.

He doesn't.

"What's wrong?" I ask groggily. I feel like I've been sleeping for days. Maybe I have. The last… *How long has it been?*

I don't know.

A week?

Two weeks?

I'm not even sure what day it is. At least the rising sun off the balcony tells me it's morning.

"I know better than to set food in the nest," Oros tells me, making me frown.

"What?" That seems strange. Why would food not be allowed…?

I nearly gag, the notion suddenly making me nauseous.

"Oh." Yeah. Food does *not* go in the nest. "You're right."

"I know." His lips quirk up a little. "I learned my lesson when I tried to feed you strawberries during the first day of your heat. You threw the bowl onto the floor and hissed at me."

I grimace. "Oh," I dumbly repeat. "I'm sorry."

"Don't be. I enjoy your directness. It makes your submission that much sweeter." He lifts the tray. "So can I tempt you to join me in the living area? I suspect you're hungry."

I run my gaze over his sculpted torso to the tray and down to his black pants. He looks fresh and clean and delicious. "I'm very hungry, yes."

He smirks. "For food, printesa mea. If you eat for me, I'll reward you with my tongue."

I shiver, liking that promise. "Okay."

Stretching again, I roll out of our nest and pause when something tightens my nipples. Glancing down has me gasping at the gold hoops piercing my flesh. Another adornment hangs from my belly button.

And there's a fourth in the hood above my clit.

I gape at that last one, my fingers automatically seeking it out.

He pierced me. I knew he wanted to. *But there?*

My possessive dragon side wanted to mark your pussy, he murmurs into my mind. *I tried to placate him with the idea of more lingerie, but he was insistent. However, if it bothers you, I can remove that one.*

My gaze snaps up to his. "No." It comes out strong. An immediate refusal. "I like your gold markings." They're almost as prominent as the crescent ones left behind by his claiming bites.

I expected two, but I somehow have three. Two on my neck and one on my breast.

He has the one I left near his heart and another on his neck.

"There's a third near my knot," he tells me, his eyes glittering with knowledge. That knowledge is either from hearing my thoughts or inspired by the memory of how I bit him down there.

I'm not sure.

But I suddenly wish I could remember sinking my teeth into that area of his body.

"We can do a reenactment later," he says, obviously listening to my thoughts.

I don't mind.

I can hear his, too.

And they're all about me, how he bathed me hours ago, then knotted me a final time in our nest. He knew I was on the verge of leaving my heat and wanted to ensure I woke up fulfilled.

He certainly accomplished that.

I feel extremely satisfied, something I ensure he knows by sharing my thoughts with him. "Why do we have three claiming marks?" I ask as I follow him into the living area.

"Two for our Drakonians, one for your wolf," he says, setting the tray down on a glass table. Then he spins to pull me into him, his arm instantly finding my waist while his opposite hand goes to my throat. "Your wolf placed that third bite near my knot, and it was so fucking hot."

He kisses me before I can reply, his tongue suddenly

dominating my mouth and leading me into dark temptation.

It doesn't matter that we've spent the last few days or weeks fucking.

I need more.

I need him.

"Mmm," he hums against my mouth. "Maybe you can eat while I play with your piercings."

A shudder works through me at the thought—a thought he turns into a reality as he moves me onto the couch and kneels between my legs.

"Pick up the water, printesa mea," he tells me, his lips lowering to the gold hoop near my clit. "Each time you swallow, I'll lick you here." He demonstrates, the metal barely grazing my sensitive nub. It's a taunt, one that teases my nerve endings and causes my thighs to clench.

I reach forward to grab the water and drink.

Oros remains true to his word, his tongue working the gold ring every time I swallow.

By the time I finish the bottle, I'm basically panting.

"Eat the fruit," he says, his words vibrating my slick flesh.

I don't question him, just do what he asks.

The bowl empties quickly, my mind more focused on his mouth than the task of chewing. Every part of me is on fire for him, my inner walls begging for friction. "Knot me."

"Not yet," he says, telling me to eat the croissant next.

I do.

But oh, moons, I'm about to combust.

Yet all he's doing is grazing my clit.

It's… it's *madness*.

Somehow, water appears. Maybe he picked up another

bottle. I don't know. However, I'm swallowing everything, and he just keeps licking.

Until finally he knocks me onto my back and climbs over me.

His pants are long gone, making me wonder if he magically blinked them away. It's not a talent I'm familiar with, and I probably just missed him removing the fabric, but I'm too caught up in the moment to worry about anything other than his cock nearing my entrance.

He doesn't give me a second longer to think, his hardness entering me in a swift punch of his hips.

And then he's fucking me.

Hard.

Fast.

Thorough thrusts.

I cling to him as he kisses me, my taste coating his tongue and now mine. It's so arousing. So titillating. So *familiar*.

This male has mastered me entirely, and I couldn't be more pleased. More thankful. *More in love.*

He's introduced me to a new world, an existence I never thought was possible. A place where I'm accepted. And not just that, but *worshipped*.

I can hear how much he cares about me, how beautifully my soul fits to his. There isn't a single part of me that he wishes could change.

Especially not my wolf.

You're perfect, he tells me. *Every part of you is perfect. Made for me. My ideal mate. My Gold Sector Princess.*

The title has me clenching around him, my heart beating in overdrive.

That's my role now.

I'm no longer an abomination. A mutt. An insignificant hybrid.

But a princess.

The Princess of Gold Sector.

Prince Oros's mate.

His chosen Omega.

I wondered if maybe this was a fairy tale before, but now I know it is. This is *my* fairy tale. And I finally understand the meaning of a happily-ever-after.

Here in Oros's arms.

Caged beneath him as he worships me with his body, loves me with his tongue, and caresses me with his hands.

This is our beginning.

Our present and future.

As the Gold Sector Prince and Princess.

Oros's knot explodes inside me as I think of those titles, his groan one I feel to my very soul.

We're connected now, not just in our physical form, but our spirit forms, too.

Mates for eternity.

Married on a plane few others can even begin to define.

And as I stare up into his alluring eyes, I feel safe. Cherished. *Loved*.

A small part of me whispers uncertainties, a part that endured too many harsh words over several formative years of my life.

But I push that negative voice away as I think, *Enough.*

I'm tired of listening to all those cruel words. The taunts. The jeers. The comments about my wolf.

She's beautiful. She's powerful in her own right. And she simply makes me unique.

There may be moments of uncertainty, ones where I question my worth, but this isn't one of those moments.

Oros palms my cheek, his long hair falling down

around his face to form a curtain of golden-blond strands around us.

"I'm going to spend every day of eternity ensuring you never have one of those moments again," he tells me, clearly having heard all my thoughts. "Because, Taliana of Gold Sector, you are more than worthy. You're a fucking Goddess, printesa mea."

He kisses me again, this time slowly and languidly as his knot continues to pulse inside me.

"You're *my* fucking Goddess," he goes on. "And someday, we're going to create a nest of pups and whelps." His mind tells me how much he wants that, his desire surprising me because part of me thought he bred me during my heat.

But he didn't.

I would sense it if we created a life.

He used protection, I realize, seeing the confirmation in his mind.

Some hazy part of me recalls questioning that early on in my heat. I wasn't sure then of what I wanted. However, hearing his yearnings now, knowing that he craves whelps *and* pups, I know I desire that, too.

My next heat probably won't occur for several months.

Or maybe it'll be during the next moon.

Given my genetics, it's hard to know for sure.

"Maybe I am Rumpelstiltskin after all," Oros muses, his eyes dancing with mirth. "I'm craving your firstborn. And second born. And third born." His eyebrows waggle, his lips curling. "In return, I'll give you however much gold you want, printesa mea. In fact, I'll give you my whole sector."

I giggle. "I think I just need your knot, Alpha."

"Mmm, you can absolutely have that, too." He presses

his hips against mine, causing said knot to spasm inside me. "Every fucking day and night."

"Sounds like utopia to me."

"Not utopia," he replies. "Just our lives." He brushes his lips against mine. "An eternity of happily-ever-afters."

"Sounds like my kind of fairy tale," I reply.

"Indeed," he agrees. "Now kiss me until my knot subsides. Then I'll take you for a flight. I want the whole sector to see their princess on my back."

"Dressed in gold?" I guess.

His lips curl. "Always, printesa mea. Always."

EPILOGUE
ONYX

I PACE THE GOLD FLOOR OF THE COURT, MY HANDS BEHIND my back.

It's a nervous tic, one I'm very aware of and do my best to keep hidden.

But the only other person in the room right now is my brother. And he already knows how I feel about this situation.

Because he feels the same way.

At any moment now, Rio's sister is going to realize her fate. Understand that her brother lied about their destination. And no doubt react to that misinformation.

"He should have told her the truth," I mutter. It goes against the grain to trick an Omega, especially like this.

"Maybe. But we don't have a full understanding of their circumstances," Oros says as he plays a gold coin through his fingers.

It's a coin he made for his mate, one I have no doubt he intends to give her as soon as he returns to their nest.

Seeing him like this is almost amusing enough to distract me from our impending meeting. He just left his mate after spending nearly ten days in bed. Yet he's clearly eager to return.

"We need to organize a coronation," he says, changing the subject away from Rio's arrival. "I want to crown Taliana in front of the sector."

I arch a brow at him. "You never wear a crown."

"No. But I like the idea of Taliana wearing one." The coin speeds up between his fingers. "I'll make one and add gold diamonds, like her belly ring."

"Belly ring?" I echo.

His eyes light up. "I pierced her."

"Oh?" Perhaps I am a bit more distracted now. "With gold?"

"Yes."

"How many times?" I ask him.

"Several," he replies vaguely. But I can tell he's pleased. "She's very thoroughly marked."

"I have no doubt that's true," I drawl, glancing at the crescent scar on his neck and the matching one on his chest. Taliana likely bears similar claiming indents in her fair skin.

Two weeks ago, that would have bothered me.

But I've embraced my brother's choice. He fell fast and hard—something I'll never understand. However, he's pleased. And that's good enough for me.

"Perhaps once this babysitting assignment is finished, we can host a coronation for my mate," he says. "Assuming we're not pulled into a battle with Obsidian Sector, anyway."

"As long as Rio upholds his promise not to share our involvement, we should be fine." Unfortunately, I'm concerned he won't uphold that promise at all.

Obsidian Sector is currently awaiting his arrival, their expectation being that he's bringing them a coveted

Omega Princess. Rio fully intends to arrive empty-handed, a fact no one other than the three of us—me, my brother, and Rio—knows.

Well, the sister will know soon, too. But she left Jasper Sector thinking that her brother had finally seen reason and was taking her to Wes.

From what Rio has said, the Omega feels strongly about upholding the blood vow her father made with the royal Alpha bloodline of Obsidian Sector.

"She's dutiful to a fault," he told me a week ago. "So getting her on the plane won't be difficult. She'll be pleased to play her part, out of respect for our father."

His tone indicated how he felt about that.

Just as my tone told him how much I disapproved of his plan to trick his sister.

I only just filled Oros in on everything yesterday. I put off Rio's arrival for as long as I could, wanting my brother to be available in case this meeting went sideways.

Because it would only be the four of us today. No Royal Court. Just me, Oros, Rio, and the Omega Princess.

"He's here," my brother says a second before I sense the power shift.

Glancing out a nearby window, I frown. "Where's his pla—"

I spin as Rio materializes in the room with a struggling female in his arms.

My gaze widens.

Then an explosion sounds somewhere in the distance.

He growls. "You'd better hope that didn't crash into anything important, Mari."

The pink-haired female growls right back at him, clearly unfazed by the Alpha's manhandling. "I hope it took out part of the sector so you'll be forced to clean it up!"

He releases a long breath, his patience clearly reaching an end. "I'm going to go check on the remains of the very expensive jet my sister just forced me to abandon mid-landing."

The female's brows come down, her profile only partially in view. "Who are you—"

He vanishes, causing her to stumble a bit.

She looks down at the gold tiles, then whirls around like she's trying to find her brother.

Only, she finds me and Oros instead. And neither of us is gazing upon her with a favorable expression.

"Welcome to Gold Sector, Princess Mari," Oros deadpans. "I can say with certainty that no one has ever made an entrance quite like that before."

She has the good grace to pale slightly.

However, it's a short-lived reaction. Because in the next breath, her pretty blue eyes narrow and she straightens her spine.

"Well, perhaps if I were a willing guest, I would have arrived by normal means. But as I'm a very *unwilling* guest, it seemed more appropriate to introduce you to the chaos I'll create should you force me to remain here."

I gape at the little hellion who just expressed absolutely no remorse for her actions. "You would rather face your dark fate in Obsidian Sector than be our esteemed guest here?"

Those alluring eyes meet mine. "I am betrothed to Alpha Wes."

"And do you know what kind of monster he is?" I ask her, still shocked by her insolence. Or maybe it's her naivety that stuns me.

"I'm an Omega Princess," she says, like that explains everything.

"I'm fully aware of who and what you are," I reply,

taking a step toward her as I weave my magic around her. "That doesn't answer my question."

"I'm his betrothed," she tries again.

"And you what?" I press. "You think that'll exempt you from his horrific preferences? That he won't sell your Omega pussy to the highest bidder? Or try to use your pure genetics in his fucked-up breeding games?"

"Onyx," my brother warns.

"No," I snap at him. "This is ridiculous. She crash-lands a fucking jet into our sector, doesn't apologize, and claims she's in her right because she'd rather be given to a monster?"

"I warned you that she has a strong sense of duty," Rio says as he reappears in the room. "The jet took out a few rocks near the shore, and it seems to have been contained to that area. I've lost a very expensive investment, but at least nothing was damaged."

Mari finally appears to be somewhat contrite. "You lied to me."

"I did," he replies. "To save your life."

"Rio—"

"No, Mari. As your Sector Prince and as your brother, I've made my decision. Accept it." He looks at me. "Good luck. I'll be in touch."

He disappears again before I can even reply, causing me to gape at Oros.

My brother simply holds up his hands and smiles. "You suggested this alliance. I look forward to seeing how it goes."

"*Oros.*"

"To echo what Rio just said, good luck," he taunts. Then the bastard fucking ashes like Rio did.

I growl.

A sound that intensifies when I feel the little hellion try to ash, too.

Her eyes widen when she realizes she's been grounded, her porcelain cheeks flaming a rosy shade of pink. "*Unleash me.*"

I snort at that. "Sweetheart, keep this up and I'll dress you in white-gold chains. Then you'll learn a whole new definition of the term *leash*."

Fuck, maybe that's what she's into.

She does want to go to Wes, after all.

"Let's go," I say, needing to put her somewhere so I can go for a long flight. "I'll show you to your room."

"Don't you mean cell?" she counters.

I sigh. "It'll certainly feel like a prison," I admit.

Because I've just taken on the role of warden.

For a very bratty, very stubborn Omega Princess.

Why the fuck did I agree to this?

Oh, right. Political alliances.

Shit.

This is going to be the hardest assignment of my life, and not just because I'm dealing with a little hellion. But because that little hellion is wrapped up in a pretty pink package, one that smells like spring flowers after a rain.

Why I notice that, I don't know.

But I'm not going to be like Oros and let an Omega's alluring scent go to my knot.

Especially not this Omega's.

Because this female is trouble.

When I take a mate, she'll be docile and sweet. Not feisty and disobedient.

"As my brother said, welcome to Gold Sector," I tell her as we enter the elevator. "My name is Onyx." I meet her bold gaze. "But you can address me as *Alpha* or *sir*."

Her eyes narrow. "How about *Asshole* instead?"

I feel her try to ash again.

This time, I'm not gentle with my *leash*.

She gasps.

I growl.

And I walk her back into the elevator wall. "If you like monsters, I can be one, little hellion." It's a lie. I'd never harm an Omega. Especially not like Wes does.

But she doesn't know that.

Nor does she realize I'll never touch her against her will, hence the reason my hands are on the wall beside her head, not on her petite form.

"Your brother left you under my care," I go on. "A mistake, honestly, since I despise your brother. So I suggest you don't push me, little one, or you might not like the consequences."

She doesn't reply. But she doesn't look away either.

After a beat, I pull back and select my floor.

Mari remains silent.

When I glance at her, I swear I see a slight sheen in her gaze. But it's gone with a blink and replaced by a determined look.

She's absolutely going to try to escape.

And I'm going to be forced to hunt her down.

Fuck. My. Life.

Thank you for reading *Gold Sector*! Onyx and Mari are up next in *Silver Sector*.

USA Today Bestselling Author Lexi C. Foss loves to play in
dark worlds, especially the ones that bite. She lives in
North Carolina with her husband and their furry children.
When not writing, she's busy crossing items off her travel
bucket list, or chasing eclipses around the globe. She's
quirky, consumes way too much coffee, and loves to swim.

Want access to the most up-to-date information for all of
Lexi's books? Sign-up for her newsletter here.

Lexi also likes to hang out with readers on Facebook in her
exclusive readers group - Join Here.

Where To Find Lexi:
www.LexiCFoss.com

ALSO BY LEXI C. FOSS

Elemental Fae Academy - Reverse Harem

Book One

Book Two

Book Three

Elemental Fae Queen

Winter Fae Queen

Hell Fae - Reverse Harem

Hell Fae Captive

Hell Fae Warden

Hell Fae Commander

Hell Fae Prince

Hell Fae King

Immortal Curse Series - Paranormal Romance

Book One: Blood Laws

Book Two: Forbidden Bonds

Book Three: Blood Heart

Book Four: Blood Bonds

Book Five: Angel Bonds

Book Six: Blood Seeker

Book Seven: Wicked Bonds

Book Eight: Blood King

Immortal Curse World - Short Stories & Bonus Fun

Elder Bonds

Blood Burden

Assassin Bonds

Mershano Empire Series - Contemporary Romance

Winter's Arrow

Bariloche Sector

Venom Island

V-Clan Series - Shifter Omegaverse

Blood Sector

Night Sector

Eclipse Sector

Kodiak Sector

Vampire Dynasty - Dark Paranormal

Violet Slays

Crossed Fates

Other Books

Scarlet Mark - Standalone Romantic Suspense

Rotanev - Standalone Poseidon Tale

Carnage Island - Standalone Reverse Harem Romance

Monsterland Mayhem - Standalone Reverse Harem Romance

Claim Me - Standalone Reverse Harem Romance

Chase Me - Standalone Omegaverse Romance